WORTHY OF TRUST
AND CONFIDENCE

Donald Brewer

TotalRecall Publications, Inc.

TotalRecall Publications, Inc.
1103 Middlecreek
Friendswood, Texas 77546
281-992-3131   281-482-5390 Fax
www.totalrecallpress.com

ISBN: 978-1-59095-055-5
UPC: 6-43977-40550-0

Printed in the United States of America with simultaneous printings in Australia, Canada, and United Kingdom.

FIRST EDITION
1   2   3   4   5   6   7   8   9   10

This book is dedicated to our six grandchildren, all of whom get to go to Walt Disney World with Mimi and Don on their fifth birthday, the last being Joshua in January of 2014.

Scott,

Best regards to a fellow history lover.

Hope you enjoy the book!

Don

Author: Donald Brewer

spent 26 years with the United States Secret Service, retiring as the Special Agent-In-Charge of the Counterfeit Division in Washington, D.C. Don spent his early years as an undercover and case agent in the Atlanta Field Office before moving to Miami, where he spent 11 years in the 1980's when Miami was the counterfeit capital of the world. In one 24-month period, he and his squad suppressed 26 counterfeit manufacturing operations. He has appeared on the Discovery Channel and the Learning Channel in episodes detailing the manufacturing of counterfeit U.S. currency. In addition, he has given speeches and made presentations regarding counterfeit U.S. currency at various conferences and seminars sponsored by Interpol and other foreign police agencies. Don has a B.A. from Furman University and an M.S. in Criminal Justice from Georgia State University. He is a member of the Association of Former Agents of the United States Secret Service, the National Association of Eagle Scouts, and the North American Peruvian Horse Association.

Don and his wife, Linda, are the proud owners of two Peruvian horses (SRR Animoso and LEA Torreon) and have ridden in a number of shows and parades.

Don is a throat cancer survivor, and after 10 years, has been declared cured. Such victories do not come without a price; Don now speaks with an electronic artificial larynx. The couple split their time between St. Simons Island, GA, and Cotopaxi, Colorado.

Acknowledgment

I would like to thank Mike Sampson, the USSS Archivist, for the photos and historical information. I would like to thank André, Sandy, Lynn, Lori, and my grandson, Stephen, for their reading, editing, and opinions. I owe thanks to my son, Brian, for his assistance. And I would like to thank my wife, Linda, for her continuing support and assistance in bringing this book to fruition.

About the Book

Worthy of Trust and Confidence is a fantasy/historical fiction book of a U.S. Secret Service case in 1898. A trio of children enter the Mousegate at Walt Disney World and each one becomes embedded with one of the three main characters. They see and feel the emotions of the characters.

They live the history

List of Characters

Maggie, Stephen and Lizzie – The trio who are given the magical badge that unlocks the Mystical Mouse Gate.

Will Scott – A Secret Service operative who leads an investigation into a counterfeit manufacturing operation in 1898 Colorado.

Miguel – Will's sidekick and lifetime friend.

Eddie Donnally – the author of the journal which details the counterfeit case. Eddie is also another Secret Service operative working out of the Washington Field Office and Will's close friend.

Lisa Butler – Owner of Cataloochee Ranch, who becomes another one of Will's partners.

PROLOGUE

Day One

"Come on, Mom. Why do we have to do this now?" asked Maggie. "We are going to Disney World tomorrow and I need to get ready."

"Because you and Stephen were assigned history assignments to do over the summer and you both have waited until the last minute, again," answered her mom.

"But Aunt Sandy . . ." started Stephen.

"Don't bother, Stephen," said Maggie. "She's made up her mind. I've been her daughter long enough to know that look."

The SUV they were riding in pulled into the driveway of a large log house sitting on a 10-acre estate lot with horse stalls and pasture.

"Mimi told you to go down in the basement and look in the large steamer trunk with Donnally on the outside, right?" asked Aunt Sandy.

"Yes, ma'am," chimed Maggie and Stephen.

"Why can't I go with you, Aunt Sandy?" asked Lizzie, Stephen's younger sister.

"You can help them with this project, too," replied Aunt Sandy. "I've got some last minute things to do before tomorrow's trip to Walt Disney World."

"Does that mean I'm in charge?" asked Lizzie, as they climbed out of the car.

"Get real, Lizzie," said Maggie.

"I'll be back at 12 noon to pick you up, so you three get busy," said Aunt Sandy.

The trio trudged up the front walk. Maggie was almost 16 and usually their de facto leader. Stephen was 15, but because of his birthday, was two grades behind Maggie at their school. Lizzie was 12 and was always taking orders from the other two—orders she frequently ignored.

The history project that was the source of their complaints had been assigned at the end of the past school year. The assistant principal of their school was a genealogy fanatic and had decided that all the students should research their family's history over the summer. Students in the same family could pool their efforts. Lizzie wasn't in the same school yet with the older two, so she was spared of having to do the assignment.

"At least we were allowed to research Mimi and Abuelo's (grandfather in Spanish) family tree," said Stephen.

"You're right. Everybody thinks we are related, but it's like by marriage or something. We're not really cousins," said Maggie.

"I don't understand why you two couldn't just talk to Mimi and Abuelo tomorrow. We're all meeting at Disney World to celebrate Josh's 5th birthday," said Lizzie. "They could probably just tell you everything you need to know."

"Because all the parents said no. This is Josh's big deal just like all of us had our trip on our 5th birthday," answered Stephen.

"Let's get this over with," said Maggie, while opening the door and leading them inside. The trio trudged down to the basement where they turned on the overhead lights that brightly illuminated the entire basement.

"Mimi said the steamer was over in the far right corner," said Stephen. "I'm with Lizzie, I thought Mimi or Abuelo would just tell some old stories."

"There it is," piped Lizzie.

The trunk looked old and was wedged in the corner by several other trunks. The trio got to work pulling trunks back and created a small work area in front of their target trunk.

"Who is this Eddie Donnally, anyway?" asked Stephen.

"I'm not sure," said Maggie, "but he must be some relative or something since Mimi sent us specifically to this trunk. Maybe she and Abuelo will tell us a good story after we see what's in the trunk."

"Well, here goes," said Stephen, unlatching the trunk and easing the top back. The trio peered into the trunk. It was packed with what looked like very old boxes, each one with a number. Sitting on the top layer was a folder that also looked old.

Maggie reached in, picked up the folder, and read, "The Journals of Eddie Donnally, Will, Lisa and Miguel, 1898. It feels like there is a book inside."

"Wow, that's really old," exclaimed Stephen.

"Hurry and open it, Mags," said Lizzie.

Maggie pulled out a leather bound volume that had a wide blue ribbon around it. Pinned in the center was a five-pointed silver star that said U.S. Secret Service.

"Wow, cool," said Stephen, reaching out and unpinning the badge.

Maggie opened to the first page and they all stared at an incomprehensible language that didn't resemble anything they had ever seen.

The overhead lights suddenly blinked out, and the trio was left in complete darkness. They felt a cool breeze, and within two to three seconds, the lights came back on, but only half as bright as before.

Lizzie squealed, and the other two stared after her at a little man who was sitting on another trunk across from them.

"Top of the morning," quipped the little man in a lilting Irish accent.

The trio was so surprised that they couldn't speak. They just stared with shocked looks on their faces.

"What's the matter with ye?" asked the little man smiling. "Cat got your tongue?"

The little man was dressed in a western style. He had on cowboy boots, blue jeans, a shirt and vest. Around his neck was a silver and turquoise four-leaf clover bolo tie. In his hand was a dark wooden cane with a shiny, lighter colored knob on the end.

"Who are you?" stammered Maggie.

"Haven't you wee ones ever heard of a leprechaun?" he asked.

"Leprechauns don't look like you," said Stephen. "They wear green suits, and a funny hat. Besides, they are not real."

"Not real!" glared the little man, raising his cane. "How would you like a rap with my shillelagh?" he asked.

Lizzie stepped forward and stuck out her hand. "Hello, sir. My name is Lizzie."

The little man stood up and shook her hand. "Pleased to meet you, and a fine lass you are. That strawberry hair brings tears to an Irishman's eyes," he replied.

"Being a leprechaun has some advantages. I already know you're Maggie and the surly one there is Stephen," he said, pointing his shillelagh. "You can call me Ace, by the way."

Maggie said, "I don't understand any of this."

"Well lass, it's like this . . ."

"Ace? What kind of name is that for a leprechaun?" interrupted Stephen defiantly.

"It's my name, lad, and you would try the patience of a saint, much less a wee leprechaun like me. I may have to give ye a taste of my shillelagh yet," barked the little man, waving his cane toward Stephen.

"As I was saying, I'm a leprechaun from a special clan. This surly one is right, though. There are some low-class leprechauns who dress in green and run around causing mischief. My clan has a proud heritage of service to special people and to preserving history, not the history you see in books or in those crazy movies. I understand you three are here to learn some real history."

"Mimi sent us to this trunk, but this book is written in some foreign language," said Maggie.

"Can you read it to us?" asked Stephen.

"Aye, I could read it since it's in me native tongue, but I'm not going to," he answered.

"I figured as much," grumbled Stephen.

"I'm going to do you one better, sonny. You three are going to live the history that's in Eddie Donnally's fine journal there," replied Ace.

"How are you going to do that, Mr. Ace?" Lizzie asked politely.

"You three are headed for a magical place tomorrow, a place

where dreams can come true. That Walt Disney was a fine lad with a great mind," said Ace with a slight grin. "Anyway, in the park is a Mystical Mouse Gate which has great power."

"I've never heard of a Mouse Gate attraction, and we've been all over the park," complained Stephen.

"Of course you've never heard of it, lad. Only someone with a mystical key can see and then enter the gate. For centuries, it was just called the gate, but once established in the park, all my clansmen started calling it the Mystical Mouse Gate," answered Ace. "I can't tell you exactly where the gate is, but once you get near it and you have the key, you will be able to see it and enter. That badge you're holding, laddie, will be your key, but you have to keep it secret."

Ace stood up and looked them each in the eyes one at a time. "Aye, I think you will have a fine adventure," he said, stepping back. Ace tapped his shillelagh on the floor and then disappeared before their eyes. The lights instantly brightened to their earlier level. "And take the book with you" they all heard in an Irish accent.

The trio all started talking at once, but a honking horn caught them by surprise.

"Geez!" exclaimed Maggie, looking at her watch. "It's been two hours."

"We don't tell anyone about this," ordered Stephen. "We'll all end up in the looney bin instead of Disney World." They all nodded in agreement and repeated together, "no one."

The trio hurried upstairs to the car, with Maggie holding the book tightly under her arm and Stephen stashing the badge in his pocket.

Day Two

The next morning, the two families met at the Nashville Airport for their flight to Orlando. Joshua, the birthday boy, was already wearing a pair of Mickey Mouse ears. Maggie, Stephen and Lizzie were sitting in three-across seats during the flight.

"You did bring the book, didn't you, Mags?" asked Stephen. "I put the badge in some socks at the bottom of my suitcase."

"Of course," she answered. "I've got the book in my back pack."

"I wonder where we will find the gate," mused Stephen.

"So, you are a believer now?" asked Lizzie.

"Yeah, yeah," replied Stephen, "at least for now, anyway."

"I'd like to have me one of those shillelaghs," said Maggie, laughing and eying Stephen. "I could put it to good use."

Mimi and Abuelo met them at baggage claim with a large courtesy van. After arriving at the hotel and putting away their luggage, everyone met in Mimi and Abuelo's room.

"You ready for the park, birthday boy?" asked Abuelo, rubbing Josh's head, which was vigorously nodding.

"Okay," barked Mimi, taking charge. "Let's get going. The park is open until midnight. Does everyone have their phones or iTouches? Stupid question," said Mimi, rhetorically. "I think you all have them glued on!"

As long as they agreed to keep a close watch on Lizzie, the trio was allowed to roam around on their own. The only requirement was to check in every hour or so with Mimi. They had wanted to talk to Mimi about the trunk, but they could never get her alone.

"It's 8 o'clock and we've been rushing all over trying to find the gate. Can't we rest for a minute?" complained Lizzie.

"Okay," said Maggie. "Let's sit on this bench and talk about where we want to go next."

"We've already been on Splash Mountain and Space Mountain and everything in between. I thought we would've found something by now," grumbled Stephen. "We're wandering around looking for a 'Mystical Mouse Gate' that a leprechaun named Ace said we would find. Talk about get real," he added, shaking his head.

"We're right here at the Haunted Mansion and there's not much of a line. Let's take a break, go in, have some fun, and not worry about looking for the gate right now," said Maggie.

"That sounds good," said Lizzie, standing up.

As the trio moved toward the Haunted Mansion, the visitor line forked. The left side went through the cemetery and the other straight to the Mansion.

"Let's go to the cemetery!" exclaimed Lizzie. "I've never been that way before."

They entered an area of fake tombstones, some sitting at crazy angles, some perfectly straight. As they walked toward the back of the cemetery, Maggie stepped up to one tombstone that was a little off by itself. She began reading it aloud: "Here lies Eddie Donnally."

Instantly, the trio was engulfed in darkness, and a shiny five-pointed star appeared on the tombstone in front of them.

"The badge is warm now," said Stephen, fishing it out of his pocket.

"Gee wiz, it's glowing too!" exclaimed Maggie.

"That must be where we put the badge!" cried Lizzie. "But I don't see any gate."

Stephen stepped forward and fitted the badge into the glowing star on the tombstone. The tombstone disappeared and was replaced by a door. There was a muted glowing white light coming from the doorway that was strangely calming.

"I would like this better if Ace were with us," said Stephen. "I wonder what he meant about "living" history."

"I liked Ace," said Lizzie, "So, I'm ready."

"Only one way to find out," said Maggie, taking each of their hands and leading them through the gate.

CHAPTER 1

Captain Will Scott and Sergeant Jonas Beard rode directly up to Colonel Martin. "The Indians that left the reservation are just over the next hill about one-third of a mile from here," reported Scott.

"Do they appear hostile?" asked Martin.

"No, they are just camped around a small spring that sits between these hills," replied Scott. "The ten horses they took with them from the reservation are grazing peacefully. We eyed them with glasses and there are no braves on watch. There are 23 in the camp."

"All right," said Martin. He disdainfully eyed Scott and Beard, who were dressed in working cowboy style clothes, and said, "You two need to stay back since you are not properly uniformed."

"If it's all right, Colonel, Sgt. Beard and I will ride east around this hill and be in position to spot any horses that might scatter," asked Scott.

"Fine," snapped the Colonel. "Just stay out of the way since neither of you is part of my detachment. You're just scouts."

"Just give us about 30 minutes before you move the column up, Sir," replied Scott, as he and Beard swung their horses away from the group.

As they rode away, Beard looked at Scott and laughed. "He really made you mad, didn't he?"

"If this wasn't the army, he would be on the ground missing some teeth," growled Scott. "I don't know whether he ignored you because you are black or because you're 'just a sergeant'!"

"Don't let it bother you," replied Jonas. "The officers that count know I'm the best horse wrangler in the Army."

As the two moved out of sight, Martin motioned to his two captains. "Have the column advance in a skirmish attack line," he ordered.

"Are we finally going to get some real action?" asked Captain Johnston.

"Yes, we are," answered Martin, as he moved into position out front and in the center of the line. "Let's go teach these Indians how the cavalry treats savages who break the rules."

Scott and Beard were about half-way to where they wanted to be when they heard the bugler sound the charge. A volley of rifle fire quickly followed. Scott and Beard could hear shouts and screams.

"What the heck!" Scott exclaimed, turning his horse and starting to canter up the hill toward the Indians. Beard was right beside him and asked, "You don't think . . ." as they crested the hill.

The sight below shocked even the two experienced veterans. Every Indian, man, woman or child appeared to be dead or wounded. There were soldiers off their mounts walking among the Indians and killing the wounded. Martin was in the middle of the camp swinging his cavalry saber over his head and urging his men on.

Scott kicked his horse into a gallop down the small hill directly toward Martin. Will saw Martin dismount and stride over to an Indian boy who appeared to be about fourteen. The boy was obviously wounded, on one knee and trying to use his arm to push himself up. The colonel kicked the boy back down and, raising his saber over his head, stabbed the boy in the middle of the chest. As the colonel pulled the bloody saber out of the boy and held it straight up, he let out a gleeful shout.

Twenty feet away, Will's horse was sliding to a stop with Will hitting the ground running. As his pistol came out, he shouted, "I'm going to kill you, you worthless, no-count murderer."

"Cap'n, Cap'n, wake up, wake up!" exclaimed Jonas Beard, shaking Scott awake. "You're having the dream again."

Scott woke staring into the worried face of Jonas Beard. "I'm sorry I had to come into your room, Captain. You were yelling 'I'm going to kill you, you no-count murderer,' at the top of your lungs. All of my boarders will want to move out," he continued.

Scott struggled back to the present and said, "I'm sorry, Jonas, I really don't have the dream much anymore."

The dream always ended at the same place. Jonas Beard, a half-length behind Will, had seen what Will was about to do and had clipped Will with the butt of his pistol. Will had dropped like a rock and woke up a day and a half later in an Army Stockade. His cellmate had been Jonas Beard. Will was charged with the attempted murder of a superior officer, and Jonas was charged with striking a superior officer.

While Will woke up with a headache, it was nothing compared to the headache that traveled up and down the Army chain-of-command. There had been a Bureau of Indian Affairs official on the reservation when the detachment returned, and he immediately telegraphed Washington about the atrocity.

The President chewed out the Secretary of the Army, and the trouble traveled downhill quickly. Will and Jonas had been released from the stockade, but confined to the Post. Colonel Martin was gone, immediately transferred to a post on the Canadian border.

After reviewing Will and Jonas' service records, the Secretary of the Army made several command decisions. He ordered Jonas transferred to his hometown of Washington, D.C. and granted him an early but full retirement.

Will Scott was a specialist in guerrilla tactics and spying on the enemy, which made him somewhat unique. The Secretary of the Army was friends with Chief Taylor of the Secret Service, so he sent Taylor a copy of Will's service record. After reviewing the records, the Chief thought Will would be a perfect operative. Will and Jonas had traveled to Washington, D.C. together and within three weeks of this incident, Jonas was retired and William Stanclift Scott was sworn in as a Secret Service Operative[1]. All in all, the Secretary of the Army was right proud of himself.

Now it was five years later, and Will was waking up in a Washington, D.C. boarding house owned by Jonas and his family. Most of the boarders didn't know it was owned by a black family. They just knew it was extremely clean and the food was outstanding.

"Do you still have the headache?" asked Jonas ruefully.

"No," answered Scott, "almost never. Besides, you and I both know that the headache saved my life. Even the Secretary of the Army couldn't have smoothed over me killing Martin,"

---

[1] The original men hired by the Secret Service were known as operatives. The title eventually became Special Agent.

added Will.

"You get dressed. Breakfast will be up in a little while," said Jonas, heading for the door.

"Hey," Will said. "You are as bow-legged as ever!"

Jonas answered with a derogatory salute as he closed the bedroom door.

Will lay in the bed and reflected on his long friendship with Jonas. It had begun when Will reported to the Fifth Cavalry Unit at Fort Smith, Arkansas as a First Lieutenant. Jonas was the Sergeant-in-charge of the horses, about the only job a black sergeant could have.

It was the love of horses that had first brought them together. Beard had worked with Army horses for years, and as his own personal joke, he tested the new junior officers by letting them pick their own horses. Most had no idea, and the ones who thought they were too good to ask for advice usually got stuck with ill-mannered, ill-tempered, rough riding mounts. Beard offered the young lieutenant his pick-of-the horses, and when Scott took his time, looked over the horses, and then picked the finest horse in the corral for his own, an instant friendship was formed—a friendship that would strengthen into something much stronger during subsequent military actions.

The black man was only 5'6" or so but was lean and wiry with coffee colored skin. His face was lined and he had some gray on his temples and in his sideburns. But his one outstanding feature was that he was profoundly bowlegged.

Enough of this, Will thought, as he levered himself out of bed and got busy dressing for the day.

CHAPTER 2

William Stanclift Scott had been a Secret Service Operative for a little over five years now and knew that he had fortunately discovered his calling in life. At 6'1", 180 lbs., he was a decent looking man, with green eyes and sandy hair. Though in his mid-thirties, his face had some lines that were prematurely there, but they complemented his overall rugged outdoorsy look. He was dressed like many Eastern businessmen. His paisley gray and silver vest was subdued; a dark gray frock coat over lighter gray trousers completed his clothes. The big difference was that nestled under one arm was a pistol in a hide-out holster. He was the kind of person people noticed, but not so different or unusually handsome or flashily dressed as to be overly remembered.

Scott stood in front of the bedroom window and stared out at 1898 Washington. After being sworn in as an operative, Will had spent a year in the D.C. office. He had worked cases in New York and Boston as well as the D.C. area. The work was interesting and there was a lot of socializing, but Will was not a city fella. He didn't really care for Washington, D.C. The political egos and the desire to line one's pocket were always butting up against the public conscience as defined by some newspaper's righteous indignation. He was constantly amazed at how the people in Washington could always so easily make black and white turn gray. Eventually, the Chief had assigned Will to work out of the Denver Office. It really wasn't much of

an office. There were five operatives and one clerk housed in the
U.S. Postal Service Building. The operatives were almost never
there since the area covered was large. Mostly, they went to
wherever there was a case.

It had taken three days to get to Washington by train, the
ultimate in modern transportation. The same trip five years
earlier would have taken a week, but his train had been pulled
by three locomotives and had featured Pullman compartments
and an elegant dining car.

He had hurried to Washington in response to a telegram:

> **Request you proceed STOP**
> **at once to Washington STOP**
> **New Case STOP**
> **Serious Problem STOP**
> **Top confidentiality utmost STOP**
> **CHIEF.**

This was not the first such telegram he had responded to,
and he looked forward to this new case with the excitement due
an unfolding mystery.

When Will arrived at Jonas' boarding house, there had been
a message instructing him to come to The Secretary of the
Treasury's Office at 11:00 am the following day. Checking his
pocket watch, he hurried downstairs to breakfast. Will was
particularly polite and friendly since several of the other guests
eyed him warily. They had obviously heard his early morning
outburst.

"The carriage you ordered is here, Captain," called Jonas
from the foyer.

"I'll let you know how long I'll be staying when I get back," said Scott, as he hurried out the door.

It was about a 20-minute ride by carriage to the Treasury building, and Will was trying to curb his excitement. The carriage was coming down "G" street when Will saw a short man pull a lady down and take off running with her purse. A beat police officer had noticed the incident and was blowing his whistle, but Will could see the officer was going toward the fallen victim.

Will yelled to the carriage driver to stop, and then he hit the ground running. The short man had a half block lead, but Will was in top physical shape and knew he could run the man down. The mugger cast a quick glance back and could see Will was gaining. The short man took a quick left at the next corner and then stopped about 20 feet down the sidewalk. When Will rounded the corner, the short man opened his coat and displayed what appeared to be the butt of a pistol. "You might want to go someplace else, mister," he hissed.

Unfortunately for him, as Will rounded the corner, he had pulled his pistol. Instead of seeing just a good samaritan, the short crook was looking into the business end of Will's pistol.

"Get your hands up," ordered Will. The man's hands shot up, and he was startled when he looked into Will's face.

"Aw, Mister Scott, I didn't know that was you," he muttered, relaxing his hands a little.

"Pinky McFadden, what do you think you're doing?" asked Will. He quickly saw that what at first appeared to be a gun butt was just a carved piece of wood. Will lowered his gun and Pinky dropped his hands.

"I was doing my usual, Mister Scott. You know I'm the best dipper in town," bragged Pinky, using slang for pickpocket.

"I thought you had some pride, Pinky," scolded Will. "I've never known you to knock a woman down."

"It really wasn't my fault," said Pinky. "The old bat . . . sorry, I mean lady, tricked me. I was in her purse slick as could be and had my hand on the money. But, she had pinned her money to her purse and when I stepped away, she felt me. All I could do was hold on to the purse and run. I really didn't mean for her to fall."

"Pinky, what am I going to do with you?" asked Scott.

"You got me fair and square," said Pinky, looking crestfallen. "But, remember how I helped you last time," said Pinky with a sly look.

"That was a long time ago, Pinky," said Scott.

"It was, Mr. Scott, but I just happen to know some micks who are making the queer and I know I could help you," said Pinky.

"You know I don't work around here anymore and you're making me late to an important meeting," growled Scott.

"I know, and a lot of people were glad to see you go," weaseled Pinky.

"This is what we're going to do, Pinky. I'm going to drag you back to that beat policeman, and he will take you to the city jail," said Will. "We are not going to tell him who I am, except to say I'm a good citizen. I'm going to talk to the men at the office, and if they are interested, somebody will be around later this evening to get you out."

"That's great, Mr. Scott. I'll really do good. I'm not making this up. You'll see," whispered Pinky.

"Give me that piece of wood so you don't get brained," ordered Scott.

Pinky handed Will the carved wood and the stolen purse.

"Is there some reason you didn't come forward with this earlier, Pinky?" asked Scott.

"Aw, Mister Scott, you know how it is," shrugged Pinky. "Besides, they are micks like me."

"All right, let's make this look good," said Scott, grabbing Pinky by the collar of his coat and lifting him on to his toes. Will marched Pinky around the corner and turned him over to the beat policeman. Fortunately for Pinky, the victim had only turned her ankle and was really happy to get her purse back.

Will left as soon as he could and was pleased to see that his hack had waited around. "Thanks," Will said to the driver as he hopped in.

"Hey, I had to wait," said the driver. "You hadn't paid the fare."

Welcome to the city, Will thought.

By the time Will got to the Treasury building, he was 30 minutes late. Rushing to the Secretary's office, he practically barged in.

"Good morning, Captain," beamed the Secretary, giving the younger man's hand a politician's squeeze and acting like he was early rather than late.

"Good morning, sir," replied Will, annoyed at being called Captain by the politician. If he had wanted to be called Captain, he would still be in the army, he thought to himself. Captain, when used by a military man, was a term of respect; when used by an appointed politician, it was just another word usually meant to butter you up.

Scott noticed the fine silk waistcoat and fancy accessories that adorned the man. Nothing but the finest, he thought.

"It's about time," growled a bearded older man standing to the left in the cavernous office. The tone of his voice belied the twinkle in his eye and the affectionate handshake he gave the younger man.

"Sorry I'm late, but I had to interrupt Pinky McFadden dipping a lady's purse," said Will. "I'll tell you all about it at headquarters, Chief, when we're done here."

The Chief was dressed like a character out of a Wild West Show. He was wearing a large Western hat with a gaudy hatband and a bright feather. His coat was subtly cut to reveal a pearl-handled revolver, and his shoulder length silver hair glistened in the lamplight. It was a characterization the Chief carefully cultivated. In a town that thrived on eccentricity and stories of the West, the Chief was a frequent topic of conversation.

Chief Taylor had been a buffalo hunter, cowboy, lawman and rancher before he made a large fortune when oil was discovered on his property in Oklahoma. His newfound wealth and a socialite wife from Philadelphia had brought him back East to the cut-throat politics of Washington, D.C. He cut a wide path in D.C., and one of his new found "friends" was Alvin T. Maddox, Secretary of The Treasury Department. Maddox had appointed Taylor as the Fourth Chief of the Secret Service, an organization ironically founded on the night President Lincoln was assassinated. The Service was originally formed at the request of President Lincoln to detect and arrest counterfeiters. In 1865, over one third of all the money in circulation was counterfeit, a not surprising fact, when just about every other bank in the country was authorized to print its own money. The success of the Secret Service in suppressing counterfeit money was well known in Washington, but it was Chief Taylor's flamboyant recitation of cases to newspaper editors and at Washington social gatherings that fascinated people.

(*Photo #1.)

John S. Bell, a former Chief of Police from Newark, New Jersey, was the fifth Chief of the Secret Service Division. The colorful Chief was well-known around Washington, D.C. for his Buffalo Bill disguise. During his tenure, the Service had 30 operatives and in a one-year period made 407 arrests for counterfeiting. Chief Bell was the inspiration for Chief Taylor.

Taylor and Maddox were an odd combination. Maddox was shorter and relished his role as a political appointee. He specialized in backroom deals and seemed to enjoy pulling strings in the background. While Taylor came from a working background, Maddox was a New England blue blood with pedigree, a college education and an arrogant air that he kept hidden most of the time.

"Will, we've got a serious problem this time!" said the Chief in a tone Scott recognized as meaningful. Taylor removed an envelope from his waistcoat pocket and placed five one hundred dollar U.S. currency notes on the desk. Opposite these, he placed five additional bills of the same denomination.

"Good Lord!" Scott muttered under his breath, as he picked up each bill, slowly examining them with a magnifying glass he took off the desk. Each of the ones on the left was almost a perfect duplicate of the ones on the right. Scott immediately knew they were the best counterfeit he had ever seen. There was not one thing he could say that identified them as counterfeit. It was more of an overall impression that gave them away. There was a line a little too thick under Monroe's portrait. The denominator was not quite distinct enough. The result to the trained eye was a bill just ever so slightly out of sync. To anyone else, the bills were perfect duplicates.

"I guess it's too much to assume that some upstanding citizen brought these in and reported his neighbor," mused Scott.

The Chief laughingly replied, "If it were that easy, I wouldn't have sent for you, I would have done it myself!"

"These things were found by accident in a money shipment to the Treasury from the Colorado National Bank in Denver. One of the clerks in the counting room here at the Treasury used to work in quality control at the Bureau of Printing and Engraving, and fortunately, he was the one verifying the shipment. He noticed the bills and showed them to his boss in an effort to embarrass the quality control checkers. The bills ended up with the Chief Engraver, and he confirmed them as counterfeit. A re-examination of the entire shipment turned up no others. With so little information about who might be involved, we haven't done anything to alert anyone," reported his Chief.

"When did this happen?" asked Scott.

"Seven days ago," replied the Chief. "Only the Chief Engraver, besides the three of us, knows anything about this. The counter just thinks he embarrassed the quality checkers and his old boss and has no clue to the significance of his discovery."

"Anything particular about this shipment that makes it different from any others?" queried Scott.

"Nothing at all," replied the Chief. "Except we have been able to determine that this money actually came from a bank in Leadville, Colorado. That area of the state is flooded with speculators, sudden gold strikes and all manner of riffraff."

"We have scheduled a routine examination of the Colorado National Bank in Leadville by Mr. Stanley Wilson, Federal Bank Examiner. The telegram was sent three days ago," advised Secretary Maddox.

Scott nodded in agreement, inwardly groaning at his upcoming roll as bank examiner. While he had done it several times in the past, the boredom and closeness associated with poring over bank records pleased Scott almost as much as the trip to the Dentist.

"Keep us posted by telegram of what you learn and where

you're headed," said the Chief.

"I will," said Scott, rising from his chair. "If necessary, I will use the standard code to relay anything I need to keep private."

"I'll meet my associate and pick up my gear and horse in Pittsville, then ride the train to Leadville. I'd say within five to six days, I should be examining the books," replied Scott.

After a round of friendly good-byes, Scott and the Chief left the Treasury building. The Chief said, "You've got a reservation tomorrow morning on the first train west. If we can't suppress this plant right away and a lot gets out, we might have to recall all the Monroe $100's."

"That would be ugly for everybody," replied Will. "I know we would get the most blame from all the politicians."

"You're not joking," said the Chief. "So tell me about Pinky McFadden. I remember he did pretty well with you last time."

Will briefly summarized his encounter with Pinky on his way to Treasury. "He will probably provide good information since we have something to hold over his head," said Scott.

"When we get to headquarters, you brief Eddie Donnally so he can get cracking on Pinky," ordered the Chief.

"That's good," said Will. "Me and Eddie did that last case with Pinky, and Eddie knows how to hold Pinky's feet to the fire. Pinky doesn't know it, but he's not being charged. When I dragged him back to the victim, he apologized and put his baby face to good use, even shed a few tears. I heard the lady tell the beat patrolman that she didn't want to press charges since she was able to get her money back. The patrolman told her he'd have Pinky put in jail for the rest of the day just to teach him a lesson."

"Fortunately, Pinky didn't hear any of that," Will continued, "and it was all I could do not to bust out laughing. Eddie can take him out tonight without any trouble, and Pinky will believe we got him out and not charged."

The Chief just laughed and shook his head. When they got to headquarters at 1310 "L" Street, the Chief went to his office and Will headed for Eddie Donnally's office.

Edward Thomas Donnally and William Stanclift Scott had been sworn in to the Secret Service together on the same day. Eddie liked to say he was senior to Will because he walked into the office first when Will held the door open.

During that first year, Eddie and Will were almost inseparable. While Will was a western outdoors kind of man, Eddie was a city fella through and through. The pair cut quite a wide swath through Washington's single ladies. Eddie was black Irish with the dark hair and blue eyes.

Will pushed through the doors marked Secret Service Washington Office, and spotted Donnally at his desk in the corner. "Hey Eddie, are counterfeiters turning themselves in at the office these days?" poked Will.

"Hey, yourself, country boy. I'm just waiting for them to come running in when they hear you are in town," poked Eddie right back.

After exchanging warm handshakes, Will sat down next to Eddie's desk.

"I think I may have something for you," said Will, and then explained the whole incident with Pinky McFadden.

"That Pinky and his baby face," laughed Eddie.

"I never identified myself to the policeman. He just thought I was a good samaritan," said Will. "Pinky will be glad to see one of his Irish brothers."

"Yeah, yeah, I'll handle it," said Eddie.   "Are you going to work it with me?"

"No, the Chief has me headed back West on an early train," answered Will.

"Must be something big," said Eddie, leaning forward expectantly.

"Can't do it, Eddie. The Chief will have to tell you about it when he's ready," replied Will.   "I got to go turn in some vouchers and get some money."

"You mean they actually pay you!" poked Eddie.

"Next time, Eddie," answered Will, as he headed for the cashier's office.

After taking care of his business, Will caught a carriage back to Jonas' boarding house. He had committed to dinner with Jonas and his wife, but Will planned a nap before dinner. He hadn't slept well. The unusual summons back East had meant something special, and anticipation of a new case kept him from sleeping, not to mention his having the dream.

Two blocks short of Jonas', Will got out of the carriage and went into a public telegraph office. Will composed a telegram:

To: Stanclift Farms STOP
Arkwright, Texas STOP
Miguel STOP
Urgent – Meet in Pittsville, CO, STOP
three days STOP
Bring horses and pack mule STOP
Mining gear STOP
Utmost secrecy required. STOP
Will

Will paid the bill and headed for his much needed nap.

CHAPTER 3

Eddie Donnally left the office shortly before five p.m. and went to get Pinky McFadden at the city jail. Donnally knew the jailers would be glad to be rid of one more mouth to feed. He was able to hustle Pinky out with almost no notice, just identifying himself to the Sergeant on duty.

When they got outside, Eddie gave Pinky a not too gentle punch on the arm. "What are you doing, Pinky, knocking a lady down? I should bust your fingers," growled Eddie.

"I told Mr. Scott it was an accident and all," weaseled Pinky. "Is Mr. Scott going to be working with us again?"

"No, he's busy with something. It's you and me and whoever else I need," stated Eddie.

Eddie led Pinky to the nearest Irish bar and got a table in the back away from any eavesdroppers. After ordering two pints in his best Irish brogue, Eddie said with no accent, "Okay, Pinky, let's have it."

"Look, Mr. Donnally, I need some guarantees," squeaked Pinky.

"The only guarantee you're getting is that if I catch you lying or not telling me the whole truth, it's right back to jail," snapped Donnally. "If you do right, this little incident can be forgotten."

Pinky sipped his beer and began to tell his story. "I know this guy. He runs with one of the gangs. He offered me some queer $20's, and they looked pretty good. I was dipping extra to raise money to buy some when Mr. Scott nabbed me."

Eddie Donnally scowled at Pinky.

"Anyway, Mr. Donnally, you know me. I was curious. One night last week, we was having some drinks and my friend told me he had to go pick up some of the queer. I sorta followed him across the river into Virginia. He went to a warehouse along the river and when he came out, he had a bag," continued Pinky.

"What makes you so sure this warehouse is where the money is being printed?" asked Donnally.

"When my friend was coming out the door, he turned to say something to somebody inside. I could hear the press running," answered Pinky.

"You know how many were inside?" asked Donnally.

"Not exactly," Pinky said. "I hung around for a little while and two guys came outside and were smoking. That's all I saw, Mr. Donnally, I swear."

Donnally turned slightly and nodded to two men at the bar. They picked up their beers and came over to sit at the table with Pinky and Donnally.

"These are two of my associates, Pinky. They are going to help me take care of your little problem," said Donnally.

Both men were about the same size, and both carried themselves like someone not to be messed with.

"Hello, Pinky," one of them said.

"Hey," exclaimed Pinky. "I remember you two guys from when I worked with Mr. Scott before."

"Yeah, do just as good this time as you did last time and things will be good for you," said the second man.

"You guys are something," said Pinky. "I didn't notice or recognize you at all until we got up close."

"Don't forget that for the future, Pinky," answered Eddie Donnally.

The group got up and went outside. Eddie motioned for a hack stationed across the street, and the carriage headed their way.

"We going tonight, Mr. Donnally?" asked Pinky.

"You didn't think I was going to let you out of my sight until we took care of business, did you?" replied Donnally.

"Step up into your carriage, your majesty," growled a man sitting up front with the driver.

"Hey, I remember you guys, too," said Pinky.

"No," said the driver. "You just think you do."

Pinky shut up and sat back in the seat.

"Which bridge, Pinky?" Eddie asked, as the carriage started moving down "E" Street.

"Take the 18th Street bridge and then turn right. The warehouse is the sixth one down," said Pinky.

Eddie Donnally smiled to himself, because he knew Pinky didn't follow anybody. He believed Pinky was too scared of the Secret Service to pass counterfeit money, but there was no doubt he would broker a deal for a little cut from both sides.

The carriage stopped at the intersection of 18th Street and a street called, appropriately enough, Warehouse Lane. All six of the men got out of the carriage, and Eddie Donnally said, "Give me your hand, Pinky." Pinky stuck out his hand and was shocked when Eddie slapped a handcuff around his wrist. Eddie quickly slipped the other cuff around a steel bar on the carriage.

"What are you doing, Mr. Donnally?" squealed Pinky.

"I just want to make sure you're where I can find you, Pinky, just in case this doesn't go right," said Donnally.

Donnally pulled up the passenger seat and handed two of his companions Winchester Model 1897 12-gauge shotguns with sawed off barrels. This same gun would come to be known as the "Trench Gun" in the Great War. He also handed out a sledge hammer.

Pinky didn't say anything, just stared. Donnally and his crew started moving slowly down the street. When they arrived at the warehouse, the upper floors were dark, but light showed in the downstairs even though the windows were papered over. There was a front door and a sliding door to the right to accommodate freight wagons.

"I went to see Judge Purdy before I left the office, and he signed the warrant. He told me just to fill in the address once we found the place," whispered Eddie.

His crew consisted of himself and four other operatives: Hardin, Todd, McKenzie and Hollander. "Let's check the sliding door first and see if it's unlocked. If it is, three of us will go in that way and two through the front door. The back door is on the river," said Donnally. "There's no way out."

As the group moved up to the sliding door, they could hear a press operating inside. They all smiled, and Eddie gently tested the sliding door. It slid easily an inch or two, enough for Eddie to know it wasn't locked.

"Okay," whispered Eddie. "Hollander and McKenzie, you check the front door." Hollander had the sledge hammer and McKenzie the 12-gauge. "If it's locked, hit it with the sledge and we'll slide the other door back," ordered Eddie.

Wilson and McKenzie slipped over to the front door and found it locked. Eddie gave them a thumbs up and Wilson hit the door hard with his sledge. The door burst inward, shattering the door frame. At the same instance, Eddie and the two other operatives slid the big door back and rushed forward. "Don't move. Federal officers!" shouted Eddie, pointing his pistol.

The two counterfeiters were so shocked, they were frozen in place. Eddie's men quickly handcuffed the two and made them sit against the wall.

Eddie looked around. "Nice operation you boys have going here, or I should say had going here."

There was a foot-operated platen press with engraved copper plates, some etching equipment, and several other items necessary to make counterfeit currency.

As Eddie stepped to the two men in custody, he exclaimed, "Forrest Arnold, what are you doing down here? New York getting too hot for you?"

"Gentlemen, I believe we have a wanted poster at the office for Mr. Arnold," added Eddie. Looking at the other man, he said, "I don't know this one, but he is probably some relative, since Forrest likes to keep everything in the family." Eying a packing crate containing several hand-engraved copper plates, Eddie said, "I see your brother has been working too. You can tell him for me that one of these days, I'll catch him in the act."

The two counterfeiters didn't say a word, just glared at the operatives, especially Eddie Donnally.

Eddie Donnally was able to keep his promise to Forrest Arnold in 1903. Using the new forensic science of latent fingerprints, he convicted Lloyd Arnold of manufacturing counterfeit currency plates in federal court.

"McKenzie, why don't you take our carriage back across the

river? I saw a ship being unloaded over there. Persuade the freight company to loan us a driver and a freight wagon to haul this stuff down to Headquarters. Tell them we'll pay, or we could commandeer their assistance, their choice," instructed Donnally.

"I'll be back soon," said McKenzie, raising his eyebrows. Eddie turned his back on the counterfeiters and made a cutting motion across his chest indicating McKenzie could cut Pinky loose. As McKenzie left, Eddie and the other operatives began stacking up the contraband so it could be hauled away.

(Photo #2, Courtesy of the U.S. Secret Service Archives)

Counterfeit Plant seized by the Secret Service in 1896.

CHAPTER 4

Will woke up from his nap just as it was getting dark. He knew Eddie and the other operatives from the office were going to have some fun. Pinky didn't volunteer information usually, but when you had something to hold over his head, he became a faucet of information. They shouldn't have any trouble. You always had to be careful, but counterfeiters were usually not a violent lot. Will wouldn't have missed the raid for anyone but Jonas, and besides the Chief had ordered him to go get packed and ready to leave on the early train.

He hurried down to the private dining room off the kitchen. "Hello, Francis," he said to the petite black woman setting the table.

"Captain," she said, as they hugged each other.

"You get prettier every time I see you," exclaimed Will. "I don't know what you see in that bow-legged old man you married."

During the year Will spent in Washington after being sworn in, he had lived at the boarding house. Jonas had married Francis within six months of their involuntary return from out West. She was a young widow with two girls ages 8 and 10.

"She sees a good-looking, distinguished gentleman," answered Jonas, coming in with bowls of food.

"Uncle Will," squealed two teenagers coming in with more food. They set the bowls down and hurried to hug Will.

"You two are turning into quite the young ladies!" exclaimed Will.

They all sat down to eat and talk like family about everything that was happening in their lives.

"Daddy Jonas says he is going to buy us two horses from Stanclift Farms," informed Josephine, the older girl.

"Josephine," barked Jonas. "Haven't I taught you anything about how to negotiate with a skinflint Scotsman?"

The whole table, even Will, howled with laughter.

Stanclift Farms was owned by Will and his brother Charles. The horses and the farm were a constant source of current pride as well as pleasant memories. His grandfather had been a blacksmith from Scotland. His love for horses burned like the furnace in which he forged the shoes. But the love of horses was not what set Walter Stanclift Scott apart from other horsemen. It was his uncanny ability to identify the desirable traits in certain horses and then breed them with each other to produce outstanding offspring. The old man had kept volumes of leather bound journals in which he detailed all the horses' bloodlines and characteristics he wanted to reproduce, all at a time when genetics and selective breeding was unknown in horses. It was a skill that had been passed down from his grandfather to his father. The family had become prosperous providing high quality horses for premium prices. The horses possessed a combination of speed, endurance and smooth gait that set them apart from others.

The family had finally settled in north Texas. The old man could never seem to settle down anywhere back east. It always seemed to get too crowded, or maybe he was searching for a part of the country that reminded him of the wild wide-open spaces of Scotland. Will had never given it too much thought since most of the moving was before he was born.

Scott had always marveled at how the skill with the breeding had been passed down from one generation to another. Thankfully, he mused, his brother possessed the skill. While Will had more natural ability with the horses when it came to riding and horsemanship, his mind could never adapt to the methodical analysis required for breeding. He just didn't think that way. Will's riding skills at putting the horses through their paces, however, enabled his brother to identify all the desirable or undesirable traits of the horses and breed accordingly.   The brotherly combination had made Stanclift Farms, one of the finest horse farms in the country, even better. It was truly a horse farm—there wasn't even one steer on the place. His father, as stubborn as his grandfather, had always said with a haughty tone "that ranches were for cows; we have a horse farm." There was no arguing with Scottish logic, even in Texas. It was a wonder that their partnership worked so well with Will having spent years in the army and then his absences caused by the Secret Service.

After supper, Francis shooed the girls upstairs, leaving Jonas and Will alone. Over whiskeys, they haggled over two horses, everything from the color to the markings and size, and finally to the price.

At 10:00 p.m., they shook hands on the deal and Will hurried upstairs to pack and try to grab some sleep before his early train. Will smiled to himself as he lay down, knowing all that haggling was for naught. There was no way he was taking Jonas' money. He owed the man his life. Even a skinflint Scotsman has a heart.

CHAPTER 5

Early the next morning, at the train station, an errand boy found Will with a message. It read, "Party last night very successful. Sorry you missed it." Eddie. Will tipped the boy and boarded the train with a bounce in his step.

Two days later, the train pulled into Pittsville, Colorado. Scott looked out the train window and saw a former railroad town that was slowly winding down. There were a thousand towns like it in the West—a place that flourished when the railroad was active and then slowly began to die. Some like Pittsville had periodic booms due to nearby mineral strikes, but most eventually would become barren ghost towns.

Scott retrieved his traveling bag and stepped down onto the small platform. His gaze searched the platform and locked on a Mexican vaquero lounging on a wide bench attached to the train station. The vaquero was dressed in khaki colored trousers flared at the bottom. He was about 5'7" and 140 lbs. His cotton work shirt was open at the neck and around his waist was a tooled leather gun belt. He was also wearing a working style sombrero and working cowboy boots, all in all, every man's image of a working Mexican cowboy. He caught Scott's gaze and rose from the bench as Scott approached.

"Buenos días, mi compadre," beamed the small wiry Mexican.

"Hello, Miguel," exclaimed Scott, exchanging a firm hand-shake with the smaller man. "How was the trip?" asked Scott.

"The train part, it was easy," replied Miguel, laughing.

Miguel, along with two horses and a Tennessee mule, had left the Stanclift Horse Farm after receiving Scott's telegraphed instructions. He had traveled by train most of the way, but the horses still had to be cared for during the trip. Miguel worked on the ranch with the horses when there was no Secret Service case, and with Scott for the government when there was. In government lingo, Scott was designated an operative and was allowed to hire and pay confidential informants on a daily basis. Miguel had proved invaluable as a partner and gatherer of information. People tended to ignore the small, quiet Mexican who listened attentively to saloon and stable conversations. These overheard conversations had, on a number of occasions, been critical to the successful prosecution of cases. At the conclusion of each case, Scott turned in vouchers detailing Miguel's work and securing his pay.

Miguel's father had worked the horses with Will's father at Stanclift Farms. But the family had gone back to Mexico when Miguel was small to be with the grandparents. Miguel never forgot the farm or his childhood friendship with Will and his brother, and on the day after his 18th birthday, he came back looking for a permanent job. Will was already in the Army and the vaquero was a perfect replacement. He was a tremendous horseman, both as a rider and trainer. It wasn't long before it was like he had never left and was accepted and treated like a member of the family.

As they headed down the street toward the livery stable, Scott described the counterfeit bills the Chief had showed him. "I swear, Miguel, I could barely tell them from genuine."

"That is not good, mi amigo. None of the business people

would ever know," exclaimed Miguel.

"I'm not even sure bank people would notice," replied Will. "If we can't put a stop to this, the Treasury might have to recall all the Monroe $100 bills."

"This money, it comes from around here?" asked Miguel.

"Not really," said Will.

"I'm going to the Colorado National Bank in Leadville as an examiner to determine the origins of the cash that went to Washington," explained Scott.

"I'll wait to hear from you before I try to get a job," said Miguel. "I can be lazy for a change."

"I'm going on the train without a horse since I'm supposed to be an Eastern bank examiner. I'll meet you at the livery stable closest to the bank, day after tomorrow," instructed Scott. "I don't think the counterfeiters are in Leadville, but it's too early to tell."

"You don't want me to travel along with you, in case of trouble?" questioned Miguel.

"No, let's go separate. There should be no trouble." said Scott. "This is only a routine bank examination."

"What do you think about this case, Señor Will? I think it's going to be very difficult and maybe much trouble," pondered Miguel, not giving Will time to reply. Scott grunted in agreement while shouldering his bag.

The two men walked to the small hotel for a light supper before turning in for the night.

Will Scott tossed and turned for a long time before falling asleep. It was ironic that he and Miguel should both have such ominous feelings about this case. Most times, cases started with people spending the counterfeit money in stores. For the western counterfeiters, this was a big problem. The majority of towns and cities were not very large and the storekeepers knew most everyone. The counterfeit money was easily traced, at least to a specific area, once it got to a bank. But this money was so good and could be distributed so easily that it was scary. Somebody was spending a lot of money and going to a great deal of effort to do this. They sure weren't going to take kindly to some lawman messing up their plans. Whatever their intentions, it was bound to be more than just passing a few counterfeit bills. He was going to have to be very careful; much of this part of the West was still a very dangerous place and a man could disappear without much notice.

The train ride into Leadville was fairly short, with only a water stop for the train at what once was a stagecoach line way station. Scott wasn't expecting and didn't notice any trouble until an average sized man wearing a dirty, brown bandana for a mask stepped through the forward train car door.

"Okay, this is a holdup!" shouted the masked bandit.

Scott stole a glance at the rear of the car where a second really big masked bandit stood, brandishing a lever action Winchester.

The shorter man wore city style clothes as opposed to that worn by ranchers or miners. He carried a Colt six-gun, which he had drawn from a cross-draw style holster. His pulled down hat and the bandana mask hid most of his features, but Scott would remember his brown hair, brown eyes and the large blue-black bruise on the thumbnail on the hand holding the gun.

The big man was dressed more like a working man. His trousers were held up by suspenders and his subdued flannel shirt was well worn. He had a large bowie knife on his belt, but he was not carrying a sidearm. The Winchester looked new; the stock was unscarred and the barrel was still a dark blue black.

"I want everybody to empty their pockets and no smart ideas," menaced the smaller bandit, moving down the aisle. He held a flour sack and each passenger deposited valuables.

Scott removed his wallet and threw it in the open flour sack.

"What's in the bag, tenderfoot?" asked the bandit, kicking the valise on the floor next to Scott.

"Only some banking records and papers," replied Scott.

"Well, I think I will just take them with me," said the bandit.

"Yeah," laughed the bigger man, "we might want to make a withdrawal from the bank."

"Take anything you want," said Scott, trying to act timid while seething inside.

Scott didn't have a gun and was glad he didn't. The bandits grabbed the remaining valuables, jumped on their waiting horses that had been ground tied off the rear of the train, and galloped out of sight.

Scott had the feeling that the two bandits were looking for someone and everything about him screamed timid Eastern bank examiner—from his plain clothes and plain glass spectacles to the bank records that were in the valise. But somebody had gone to a lot of trouble to hold up the train and find out what he looked like. The short bandit had looked the passengers over as he moved down the aisle, and unlike most bandits, was more interested in the people than their valuables.

The rest of the trip to Leadville was uneventful. The conductor was in an uproar over the holdup, taking it as a personal affront that someone had robbed the passengers on his train. None of the other cars had been bothered, and most of the other passengers had only tossed something of little value into the bandit's bag since neither bandit had really bothered to check their victims. None of the other passengers seemed to think the bandits were anything but stupid, and many of the men joked about the bandits' ineptness. Scott knew better. There was no doubt in his mind that they knew who to look for when they got on the train. Scott believed the outlaws were trying to verify his identity as Stanley Wilson, bank examiner, and get a good look at him. There was no doubt in Scott's mind that if the two suspected him to be a Secret Service Operative, and if he had acted, there would not only have been a robbery, but also a murder.

On the positive side, they had no idea about Miguel. Thank goodness they hadn't traveled together.

Scott pushed these thoughts from his mind as he retrieved his other traveling bag and stepped off the train onto the platform. He immediately saw the conductor rushing toward him with a deputy Sheriff in close pursuit.

"This is the man who lost his bag," blurted the conductor.

"Was your stuff real valuable, Mr. Wilson?" asked the deputy after glancing at the card Scott had produced.

"Not at all. It was just work papers, mostly blank," replied Scott. "Those two will surely be surprised when they take the time to look."

"These fellas don't exactly sound like the James gang," said the deputy, turning away from Scott, directing his comment to the conductor.

"Well, I expect you to capture them, no matter who it is," snorted the indignant conductor.

"It was probably just a couple of fellas down and out," replied the deputy. "They didn't exactly act like they were used to robbing trains. Surely, they're halfway out of the territory by now." Scott left the two men in animated conversation and headed forward to locate the bank before too many questions were asked.

CHAPTER 6

It was easily the most formidable building in town. The entire structure was brick and there were thick shutters that were obviously shut tight at night. The bank reeked of solidness and would have looked perfectly at home in Boston or Washington. It contrasted sharply with the rest of the western town's architecture of rough-hewn wood and clapboard.

There were several dozen streets in town and just about everything a person could want or need was available. Some might even call it more a city than a town. It was not built around one particular enterprise. There was the railroad, some ranching, some mining, a little farming, and all the support businesses that went with it. There was an air of permanence that was missing in a lot of western towns, towns that would eventually disappear. Leadville, as its name inadvertently implied, would be around for a while, despite its origins as a mining town.

The people at the bank were very apologetic about the train robbery. News of it had traveled fast.

"I can assure you this doesn't happen very often these days, young man," said Mr. Franklin Pierce, the President of the bank.

"I'm very glad," said Scott, "it was quite scary."

Franklin Pierce was dressed conservatively but expensively in city style clothes. He wore glasses, which he had a habit of frequently looking over. Scott knew that he had a competent reputation as a banker and was more than just a branch bank manager. His wife was a granddaughter of one of the founders of the Colorado National Bank, and Pierce had a bright future. "While you're here, you can work with Mr. Ben Johnston, our assistant manager," advised Pierce, who made short work of introducing Scott to Johnston, and showing him to a small cubicle off the lobby where the undercover examiner could work. It was obvious Pierce had little use for, and a not very high opinion of, a bank examiner.

Johnston was an average size man, whose main skill in the banking business, Scott expected, was his kinship to Franklin Pierce's wife. A relationship Pierce was quick to point out when making introductions. The pot calling the kettle black, thought Scott.

Will spent the rest of the afternoon compiling a list of the banking records he wished to review and was pleasantly surprised to learn that Ben Johnston had already pulled many of the ledgers he needed.

"It's apparent, Ben, that despite your family relationship, you are very knowledgeable in banking," praised Scott.

"I'm glad somebody has the sense to notice out here. I spent some time back East in banking in addition to my schooling. All the people out here seem to notice are cows, silver and gold. No one seems to appreciate all the businessmen here in town," huffed Johnston, retreating to his office and ledgers.

It was good news and bad news for Scott. Johnston was obviously competent, so Will would have to carefully go through the bank examining motions to keep from alerting Johnston to his real investigative mission.

The rest of the day, and all the next day, Scott spent reviewing cash shipments to and from the bank, looking for something unusual or some discrepancy.   Unfortunately, nothing was obvious. The records taken in the holdup had just been cover, but it would have been nice to compare them with the bank's, just in case. Scott didn't really give this theory much thought at all. He knew the people he was looking for were much too good to be caught that easily.

CHAPTER 7

The sun was setting as Scott slipped out the back side of his hotel and headed down a side street for the livery stable. He was careful to make sure no one was watching or following him.

The big man with the nearly new Winchester leaned against the side of a building with a good view of the front of the livery stable. This was the second day he had been there at dusk watching. He didn't really want to be there, but his boss insisted that this was the best place to find out who that nosy lawman had for a partner. If it had been up to him, he would have just shot him on the train, but the boss had just wanted him identified. He didn't understand why it was okay to shoot one now, but the boss said now would not upset the timetable, whatever that meant. The big man didn't care. He was just looking forward to shooting someone.

It was almost dark and he could leave, but then he caught sight of that lawman moving toward the livery stable. The sneaky devil was carefully noticing all his surroundings and acting nothing like a sissy bank examiner. The big man knew the boss had been right that anyone trying to follow this man would surely be noticed. He stood motionless and watched.

"Buenos tardes, Señor Will," said Miguel, standing just inside the barn's double door. "The stable hand has gone to a saloon, so there is no one here but us. It's obvious from the way you approached that there has already been trouble."

"I should have known you'd be watching," laughed Scott. "The train was held up and the bank records I was carrying were stolen. They were obviously laying for me, but I think all they wanted to do was get a good look at me. It was odd. There were two bandits. One of them was big, well over six feet and heavy. The other was maybe 5′ 7″ and slight. The big one carried a real nice and new lever action Winchester. It looked like the latest model. I don't believe there would be too awful many of them out here yet! It might be worth keeping an eye out for."

"The records are no help to them, no?" asked Miguel.

"No, they probably just wanted to make sure that I was truly acting as a bank examiner, and those records should convince them of that. But somebody at the bank must be involved or told somebody that's involved about the bank examiner coming out for an audit," replied Scott.

"Have you found anything at the bank?" queried the Mexican.

"Nothing really. The bank receives a lot of silver and gold from several mining companies and independent assayers. They send a lot of currency out to Silver Creek and Glenrock. The bank has smaller branch offices in Glenrock and Silver Creek and most of the cash both going and coming seems to pass through these branches, all of which is very interesting given the size of the town, but may mean absolutely nothing," related Scott.

"You want me to head for the mining towns?" asked Miguel.

"No, give me two more days at the bank and then we'll ride for the mines," related Scott, bending down to pick up a curry brush for his horse.

The shot slammed chest-high into a barn post, showering Scott with splinters. Miguel crouched and fired two quick shots with his pistol at the corner of the building, where he had seen the muzzle flash of the attacker. The surprise had been too sudden, and they both heard the running strides of their attacker.

"Are you all right, Miguel?" panted Scott, breathless from the near miss.

"Sí, amigo, but who would do such a thing? No one is supposed to know we're here," stated Miguel.

"Well, somebody must know something, and they're sure taking exception to what should be a harmless bank examiner from back East," marveled Scott. "Let's get out of here, before somebody comes to check on the shots," said Scott. "I'll meet you here again in two days around 11:00 a.m., since that's when the daily train leaves, and be careful. Whoever it is has now seen us together."

"You too, mi amigo," breathed Miguel as the two friends separated into the darkness.

The man with the new Winchester went up the back stairs of the high-class boarding house. He gave a soft knock and the door was quickly opened.

"What happened?" asked the man he called boss.

"They were at the livery stable. I was watching, but his partner was inside and I never got a look at him. I had him dead in my sights, even though it was dark, but he ducked just as I pulled the trigger."

"Are you sure you missed?" asked the boss.

"Oh yeah, and his partner snapped off two shots that were way too close," replied the big man.

"Anybody see you?" asked the other.

"No, there was nobody around."

"Well, no matter. I'm sure we'll get another chance," said his boss. "Can you recognize his partner?"

"No, he is a sneaky devil, too. All I could tell is that he's not real big. I never saw him arrive, and I was keeping a good watch."

The boss was frustrated, but he and the big man had been together a long time, and if anyone could have gotten the Secret Service operative, it would have been him. He was confident the next time would be different, so he let the matter go for now.

The next two days were a real strain for Scott. He didn't need to look at any more records, but he needed a look at some of the bank's money. The trick was how to do it. A bank examiner didn't just ask to examine a bank's money for counterfeit.

After lunch on the second day, however, he got a lucky break when he heard Ben Johnston addressing the only female worker at the bank.

"Miss Jones," said Mr. Johnston, "would you mind staying a little late this afternoon? There is a cash shipment coming from the Silver Creek branch. It was supposed to be before noon, but it's been delayed by a rock slide."

Miss Jones, the ever-dutiful employee, reluctantly agreed.

"Excuse me, Mr. Johnston," said Scott, "I am pretty well finished. I'll be glad to assist Miss Jones in verifying the shipment."

Miss Jones, an aspiring spinster, immediately perked up and flashed a smile at Scott.

"That would be excellent, Mr. Wilson. My wife expects me

to attend a tea for the Ladies Auxiliary, and she will never believe I had to be here at the bank. I'll come back and close up the vault after the tea," beamed Mr. Johnston. "Please just wait for me."

What had seemed to be a lucky break, however, just turned into a long frustrating afternoon. Not only did Scott not discover a single counterfeit bill in the shipment, but he had to contend with nonstop chattering of the persistent Miss Jones. When Johnston finally returned, Scott bade them both good-bye and bolted like a spooked horse for the hotel.

The next day, Scott checked out of the hotel and ate a leisurely breakfast at a local cafe on the main street. He ultimately made his way to the bank and delivered a glowing account of his bank examination to Franklin Pierce, Bank President. He spoke highly of Mr. Johnston and Miss Jones, and after saying a quick farewell to the two employees, headed for the train station. Taking a wandering, circuitous route, he arrived at the train station and mingled with the traveling passengers, which was a surprisingly large group. Scott wandered through the crowd, ultimately slipping unnoticed off the platform, down a side street, and finally arriving at the livery stable.

Miguel was standing in the nearest stall with two horses saddled and ready to ride. Alongside was a dark, big-eared pack mule, slowly eating a carrot out of Miguel's hand.

"Vámanos, Señor Will, I'm tired of this place," complained Miguel. "I was always looking backwards."

"I'm raring to go, too," said Scott, stepping into a stall and quickly changing into his riding clothes and boots and stowing his examiner clothes in a mule pack.

"The big problem is, I don't have a clue as to why we're going where we are, except that it's on a list," groaned Will.

"There was no more dinero falso in the bank?" wondered Miguel.

"Not the first bit," said Scott. "The answer was probably there, I just couldn't see it."

"No, mi amigo, the answer was not there, a trail maybe, but not the answer. Only God is that lucky," laughed Miguel, causing Scott to grin with him. Miguel always seemed to have a feel for things that defied any specific facts or circumstances. It had happened so many times in the past that Scott didn't try to figure it out, he just went with it.

It had been almost ten days since the night Scott examined the original five counterfeit bills. They had ridden a few miles from Leadville toward Denver and away from their ultimate destination, all the while carefully checking their back trail. Just before dark, they made camp. While Miguel fixed their supper, Scott climbed a nearby telegraph pole and, using an Army field telegraph key, sent his message to Washington.

> **Bank exam complete STOP**
> **shipment from mining areas STOP**
> **proceeding to Silver Creek/Glenrock STOP**
> **Information leak certain STOP**
> **Everything okay STOP**
> **Enemy unknown STOP**
> **Scott.**

The army telegraph code Scott used assured that the telegraph operator's up-line wasted no time in forwarding the message directly to the Chief.

CHAPTER 8

The telegram was on the Chief's desk the next morning when he got to the office. After reading it, he took a match out of his desk drawer and burned it. While the Chief was relieved that Will and Miguel were okay, the mention of an information leak immediately raised his blood pressure.

The Chief took a few deep breaths and then bellowed to his secretary, "Find Eddie Donnally and get him up here right away."

The order was hurriedly relayed to the downstairs Washington Office, and Eddie Donnally reported to the Chief's office within the hour. The Chief had spent the time waiting for Donnally in serious contemplation.

"Good morning, Chief," said Eddie.

"Tell my secretary to go for a long coffee break and then shut the door," ordered the Chief.

Eddie had worked closely with the Chief and knew that something big was brewing. The Chief stood up and placed ten Monroe $100 bills on his desk, five on one side and five on the other.

Eddie quickly identified the ones on the left as genuine. He picked up one of the $100 bills on the right. "Sweet Jesus!" Eddie exclaimed. "Is this why Will was back here so suddenly?" asked Eddie.

"Yes, it is, Eddie. These bills came from a bank in Colorado," advised the Chief. "I just got a disturbing telegram from Will saying there has been an information leak. He and Miguel are okay, but this is very serious. Only the Secretary, the Chief Engraver and I knew of this counterfeit. We all agreed that no one else could learn of the counterfeit."

"I know you didn't tell anybody, Chief, so that leaves two suspects," answered Eddie. "Now I understand why Will couldn't tell me about it."

"I have the only five of these counterfeit notes that have appeared, so I know it hasn't been shown around," countered the Chief.

"You can't believe it's The Secretary. I know he's a jackass, but jeez," said Eddie.

"He's not my first suspect since anything bad that happens relating to the Treasury department would put him on the hot seat with any number of politicians," answered the Chief.

"You want me to start doing some checking on the Chief Engraver?" asked Eddie.

"Use all the men you need. I want him watched full-time for the next several days. If he's gambling, smoking opium, drinking, chasing women, I want to know it," ordered the Chief. "Nobody can know why!"

"You know I'm friendly with a lot of people, men and women, over there at the BEP. I'll buy a few pints and maybe a dinner or two. People love to talk about their bosses. Present company excluded, of course, Chief," laughed Eddie.

The Chief just sort of growled and waved Eddie out of his office.

CHAPTER 9

Eddie Donnally was sitting in the Chief's office when the Chief strolled in first thing in the morning.

"Top of the morning, Chief," said Eddie.

"Save that blarney for somebody else. Please tell me this morning, unlike the last five, that you have something," grumbled the Chief.

"It's been five days and we got nothing. This guy is as clean as can be. He's nice to his kids, his wife, his neighbors and little old ladies," joked Eddie. "I think we both know where we have got to go now."

"You're right," said the Chief. "I knew it a couple of days ago, but I've just been avoiding it." The Chief unlocked a desk drawer and passed a written sheet over to Eddie.

"Here are all the particulars on the Secretary," said the Chief. "I wrote everything out myself to keep anyone else from knowing what we are doing."

"Investigating any politician, especially in this town, is asking for trouble. Any hint of trouble, the weasels all stick together and blame somebody else even though they really hate each other," warned Eddie.

"We're not going to do much here," said the Chief. "He's keeping a low profile, so if he is involved, the answer to this is somewhere in his past. He went to school up in New Haven. Get up there and do some digging. My wife and I were at one of the endless social events here a while back and were sitting at the table with the Secretary and his wife. His wife joked about him being a real rascal at school and nobody he knew then would believe where he is now. Everybody was drinking and laughing, but just for a second, I saw a mean, nasty look. You know what I mean," said the Chief. "It wasn't directed at his wife, and he laughed, but he quickly changed the subject."

"I do know that look you recognized, Chief. It's just something you know and recognize but there are really no words to describe it," answered Eddie.

"I've talked to a bunch of people from the BEP, and as you would expect, nobody said anything bad about the Chief Engraver. However, I did get wind of one oddity. About a month or so ago, the BEP security was about to arrest two brothers for stealing. Funny thing is, they just up and disappeared. One was an engraver and the other was a pressman. They were Swiss immigrants who spoke with pretty distinct German accents," reported Eddie.

"Those idiots," said the Chief. "They should have let us know."

"You know how they are about keeping stuff quiet, Chief," answered Eddie. "They avoid publicity like the plague!"

"Did they do any follow-up or was it just good riddance?" asked the Chief.

"I couldn't get too many details, but I'm pretty sure it was just good riddance," answered Eddie. "I did get where they were living, so I'll get one of the boys working on that just in case. I'll go by the house, grab some clothes and catch the next train to New Haven," said Eddie.

"Will and Miguel are out there with no idea of who the crooks are, and I suspect the crooks know more about us than we do about them," worried the Chief.

"I know," said Eddie. "I'll emphasize how precarious the position Will and Miguel are stuck in, with all the boys, without telling them about the quality of the counterfeit."

"Get going. Let me know by code, or if it's too involved, get right back here. On second thought, I don't want anybody to notice you're telegraphing from New Haven. Just get it done and get back as quick as you can," ordered the Chief.

Eddie grabbed his notes and hit the door at a quick pace.

CHAPTER 10

Four days after leaving Leadville, Will and Miguel ambled into Glenrock, tired but confident they were not being followed. The trip had really taken a half-day longer than it should—with their back tracking and scanning of the countryside.

"You know the reason we're not being followed is that we are on a wild goose chase, don't you?" asked Scott.

"We'll see," said Miguel, with the conviction of one who knows he's right.

Will Scott hoped his Mexican friend's faith was not misplaced.

Glenrock was a booming town in a booming area. It was a true town with several hotels, permanent businesses built on trade with the nearby mining camps and large ranches. There were cowboys, miners, and those who were some of both. It was the jumping off point—an oasis in the middle of vast mountainous places.

After stabling their horses and the pack mule, Scott and Miguel checked into a hotel populated with miners and cattle buyers. It was a working man's place, just a little more private than a short term boarding house, but not much.

With a fine steak meal under their belts, the two friends angled across the street to a saloon where lights blazed and a piano tinkled.

They sidled up to the bar and Scott ordered a couple of

whiskeys. "Hey, don't I know you from somewhere, Mister?" said a man standing behind Scott and eying him in the mirror.

"Unless you've been up in the mountains, it's not likely you know me," replied Scott, slowly lowering his drink.

"I guess you just look like somebody else," said the man, the animosity slowing leaving his face. It was replaced by a hustler's beaming smile.

"You fellas bring in a pretty good stake?" asked the man.

"We can't complain," replied Scott.

"Well, if you're tired of digging in the dirt, my boss is in the claim verifying business, among other things," offered the stranger, fishing a card out of his pocket inscribed with the name Two Aces Cattle and Mining Company, Andrew White, President. "I'm Al Frederick," said the man, sticking out his hand.

"I'm Will Scott, and this is Miguel Fernandez," said Scott. "I think we're going to find some more gold, and when we do, I'm going to come looking for you to buy, but it's gonna cost you!" offered Scott, giving the hand a firm grip.

"Don't forget," said Frederick, sliding down the bar and engaging two more newcomers in a conversation about mining.

"Miguel, I hate to admit it, but you were right again," offered Scott. "Mr. Frederick is one of the robbers from the train. We better get out of here before he connects it all together," said Scott, throwing down the last of his drink.

"Vámanos," breathed Miguel, as they headed for the door.

Once outside, they quickly crossed the street and ducked into the first alley they reached. When, after five minutes, no one appeared to be following them, they both sighed with relief.

"Señor Will, perhaps now you will agree that we are in the

right place to continue our search," grinned the Mexican.

"We're here, right in the middle of the frying pan," replied Scott. "But he obviously is not the one who shot at us in Leadville."

"Perhaps they would not recognize us," asked Miguel, lighting up one of the cheroots he favored.

"I don't know," replied Scott, reflecting on his appearance as a tenderfoot Eastern bank examiner in Leadville and his current prospector clothes and four-day beard. "We are a pretty common looking pair," laughed Scott, the tension easing. "Without the clear glass spectacles, I do look a little different."

"He was the hombre grande from the train?" asked Miguel.

"No, he was the smaller of the two and he was wearing a mask on the train, but I'm sure it was him. He had that bruise on his thumbnail," replied Will. "It was probably his friend we met in Leadville. Tomorrow, let's do a little scouting of the Two Aces Cattle Company and see what we can see."

"I'll follow anybody that leaves and you watch who comes and goes from the office," replied Scott, as they headed for the hotel and a good night's sleep.

CHAPTER 11

The morning was clear and chilly, one of those days that was too warm for winter, but not quite warm enough for spring. Scott found himself a spot where he could see the front of the office of the Two Aces Cattle and Mining Company. The company's name was on the front window, just like most of the other businesses in town. There was nothing unusual about the office. One good thing was that it was next to an alley and had a side door instead of a rear door. It was three doors down from the bank and across the street from one of the general stores. There was a lot of hustle and bustle in the area, what with horses, wagons and people doing bank business, in addition to the general store. Scott had no trouble settling in on a step across from the Two Aces. The warm sun lulled Scott into a dreamy complacent state that almost prevented him from noticing Al Frederick coming out of the front door of the business. Frederick was dressed in work clothes like most of the other people in town, but the man he was talking to was resplendent. The man was tall with white hair and mustache that gave him a benign, yet wise appearance. The black morning coat was contrasted with gray pants, pin-stripe vest, (gold chain, of course) and beautiful hand-tooled black boots that had never touched horse manure. While Scott couldn't overhear the conversation, he could tell from Frederick's gesturing that this must be Andrew White, President of Two Aces. Frederick finished talking to White and began to stroll down the main street. Despite all the people, Scott was able to keep up with Frederick without trouble, on the opposite side of the street. Frederick didn't seem in any hurry and spoke to several men and women as he walked along, obviously a fairly well-known resident. Scott's quarry ended up at the end of the street and entered the office of the Banton Freight Company.

There was an office in the front of the building with what looked like a freight unloading dock and a storage area in the back. To the left of the building were the corrals for the horses and mules, and several half loaded wagons were in sight towards the back of the building.

Scott could see Frederick through the front window of the office talking with who appeared to be the person in charge. The man appeared to be showing Frederick a schedule.

Scott strode quickly across the street, dodging a couple of horses, and was able to stand out of sight by the open door.

"I received a telegram from the Ft. Gordon way station, Mr. Frederick. Your shipment should be in before dark. I'll have my men unload it the instant it arrives," said the freight company manager.

"Don't bother unloading it," said Frederick, "I'll have my men here in the morning to take care of things. That's important mining equipment, you know, and I don't want it damaged by some drunk mule-skinner."

"I understand, Mr. Frederick," assured the manager. "I'll personally make sure the wagon is secure in the freight barn."

Scott stepped around the corner of the building and circled around the corrals and came back out on the sidewalk, just in time to see Frederick's back disappear into the Orleans Restaurant.

Scott headed back up the street to find Miguel and see if he had seen anything interesting happening at the Two Aces office. He spotted Miguel hunkered down in an alley 100 yards south of the Two Aces. Scott walked into the alley, and Miguel joined him behind the building a few minutes later.

"So, Señor Will, you have learned something. I can see the gleam in your eye, no?" asked Miguel.

"Maybe. Frederick went down to the freight office and I was able to overhear that he's expecting a shipment of mining equipment tonight," replied Scott.

"Your time was much more rewarding, Señor Will. The fancy man did nothing but talk to all the people passing by. He has a very good job," grinned Miguel.

"You mean there was no business going on there?" asked Scott.

"It looks like a business, but this morning it does not act like one," replied Miguel.

"H'mmm," mused Scott. "I think we are going to have to do some night work and see what these hombres are mining."

They split up, with Will becoming familiar with one end of town and Miguel familiar with the other end. It was a practice they had perfected many times before. Each man mentally noted escape routes, good hiding places and places to avoid if they were forced to move in a hurry day or night. While it would have been ideal if they both could have known the whole town, this method kept people from seeing them together but still allowed each to gather a lot of information.

The moon had not come up as Miguel and Scott moseyed down the back stairs of the hotel. They came out of the alley and headed toward the freight company, keeping to the shadows as much as possible. There was a lot of activity around the three saloons, but no one noticed the pair as they made their way to the freight company.

"You watch the front, and I'll circle the building to see if there is a night guard," said Scott.

"All right," replied Miguel, crouching down by the corner of a neighboring building.

"I'll whistle if there's no one around," said Scott.

He slowly circled the building but was relieved to find no one on guard. Scott used his cupped hand to hoot like a night owl and slowly edged around several buildings back to the spot where Miguel was crouched.

"Los niños would have recognized that as a gringo hoot owl," grinned Miguel, breaking the tension. Miguel, Will and his brother Charles had practiced making bird calls for years as kids.

"Let's go," said Scott, laughing under his breath. "There's a window on the far side that we might can open."

There was no warning cry or shout as they reached the side of the building and the window. Even the horses and mules remained quiet and barely noticed the pair. Miguel inserted his thin-bladed knife, and with a little wiggling, opened the latch. Scott pulled a nearby bale of hay underneath the window and easily climbed through. He gave Miguel a hand up and then quietly shut the window.

The barn smelled of freshly sawed wood and compared to the cool night, the air was warm. There were a half dozen freight wagons inside, some half full, several others full of goods and covered by tarps. There was a stack of hay bales on the far side of the barn, as well as several other bales scattered around.

"It should be one of these loaded ones, the way they were talking," whispered Scott.

Miguel quickly lit a miner's candle lamp, which cast a small three foot circle of light. Scott in the meantime stacked two more bales of hay in front of the window, effectively blocking all light from escaping.

"Will, look at this," hissed Miguel, lifting up the end of a tarp. Inside the wagon were tins of what appeared to be lard cans. Each can had brown paper glued to its side and there was no stenciling of any kind on the cans.

Scott pulled out his boot knife and carefully pried the lid off of one of the cans. The pungent smell of printing ink brought a quick grin to them both.

"We have found the jackpot, no?" whispered Miguel.

"I don't think we need to wonder what color this stuff is," answered Scott. He resealed the lid on the ink tin, careful not to spill any. "I wonder why this load wasn't covered and lashed down," mused Scott.

Just as Scott was stepping off the wagon, he and Miguel both heard approaching noises. Quickly extinguishing the miner's candle, they ran to the far side of the freight barn and were safely hidden among the bales of hay by the time the doors swung open.

The two men had obviously spent some time in the saloon, but they went straight to the ink wagon and threw back the tarp covering. After satisfying themselves that everything was okay, the two men checked another wagon that was completely tarped over, tightening the rope rigging.

"You want me to tighten and rig this other one?" asked one

of the men.

"No, the boss took something off of it and said just leave it until in the morning," said the other. "This shipment is not as big as the others."

Scott adjusted his position slightly in order to see the two men, but their faces were partly covered by their cowboy hats, and the small lantern they were carrying did little to light their faces.

"Jake, you think that little redhead will take me home with her tonight?" asked one of the men.

"Depends if you got a gold piece in your pocket," said Jake.

"C'mon, Jake, you know she ain't like that," complained an obviously younger man.

"Look, sonny, whatever you do, you meet me in front of the saloon at 11 o'clock, so we can check this stuff again. I don't like stomping around here in the dark by myself, and that Simpkins is too mean for me to cross. If something happened to this stuff, whatever it is, he'd cut us from ear to ear," groused Jake.

"Ok, ok," snorted the young man, as they headed for the barn door. "What do you think ever happened to Douglas and Barney? It was kind of strange, them up and disappearing like that."

The older man stopped. "You listen to me. Don't ever mention them to anybody. Being nosy can get a man in real trouble around here."

Miguel and Scott waited five minutes before moving, in case the two came right back for something.

"Is nothing but watchdogs," snorted Miguel, helping Scott move the hay bales away from the window.

"Yeah, but Simpkins is obviously some mean hombre that

we don't know, and since we haven't seen him yet, maybe Simpkins is the other man from the train," mused Scott. "I'm positive neither of those two was the other pretend train robber."

"Es muy importante," said Miguel, "we follow these wagons home, yes?"

"Sí," replied Scott, marveling to himself at Miguel's mixed command of the English language and his own ability to understand it and occasionally slip into speaking it himself.

CHAPTER 12

Miguel and Scott were up and out of the hotel before dawn. Scott paid the night clerk while Miguel retrieved their horses and the pack mule from the livery stable.

"Señor Will, do you think these men are the ones who make the bad money?" asked Miguel.

"Not a chance these fellows are making it, but the people getting the supplies surely are," said Will.

"It was green ink in the wagons, no?" asked Miguel.

"Yes and no," said Will. "You can't just go back East and tell someone you want money green ink. Usually these crooks mix the ink to their own formulas to come up with the right color. The color on these counterfeits is almost perfect. These outlaws really know what they are doing!" exclaimed Scott. "Funny thing is nobody we've seen yet appears to have anything like the skill to make this quality of counterfeit. Another thing I don't like is the quantity of their printing supplies. They can make huge piles of money with all the stuff they are shipping."

Scott positioned himself in the alleyway across from the freight company while Miguel took their horses and mule further down the street behind some new building still under construction. In the slowly dawning sun, Scott could see and hear drovers moving about the freight yard, waking up balky mules and hitching up wagons. He didn't have to wait long before he saw Al Frederick strolling down the wooden sidewalk accompanied by a hulking big man carrying a short-barreled shotgun. They were definitely the two from the train; the only thing missing was the fancy rifle. The big man was dressed like a freight driver, and in addition to the shotgun, he was carrying a big muleskinner knife with what looked like a 10-inch blade and a long-barreled, heavy caliber pistol. Scott knew that type of weapon and had seen the kind of damage it could inflict. The shooter didn't have to be good, just close. The big man was nothing but trouble, thought Scott. Scott retreated down the alley and around the back of the building to Miguel. "Let's ride, compadre. The big man and Frederick are at the barn. The wagons should be moving out shortly," said Scott.

"You think this big man is the mean one called Simpkins?" asked Miguel.

"My friend, based on his looks, that is one mean man. It must be Simpkins," replied Scott.

The two friends picked a vantage point several miles outside of town on the trail so they could see which way the wagons headed. The field glasses would help them pick out all the details without being close. Scott was pretty sure they would take the right fork which would lead them thirty miles over two mountain passes to Silver Creek. As soon as they knew the wagons' direction, Scott planned to ride down the trail the other way toward the valley. There, he would intercept the telegraph lines so he could send a message to Washington. Miguel would have no trouble tracking the slow moving wagons until Scott returned. Scott spent the time waiting and taking some supplies off the pack mule and storing it in his saddlebags. He planned on making a cold one-night camp so he could catch up to Miguel as soon as possible. He had no sooner finished, when Miguel gave a low whistle from his perch atop a jumble of boulders.

"They are coming, Señor Will!" exclaimed Miguel, picking up the field glasses.

The two wagons rumbled down the road and took the right fork just as Scott had figured. Simpkins was driving the lead wagon, while another man was driving the second. Al Fredericks was riding with Simpkins, and Scott figured the man riding in the second wagon and the driver were the two men they had overheard the night before. Both wagons had a horse tied to the back, meaning that Simpkins and Fredericks were probably coming back separately. The horse tied to the second wagon had a rifle scabbard with the new Winchester Will had seen on the train.

As soon as the wagons rolled out of sight, the two friends climbed down from the boulders and mounted their horses.

"I'll rendezvous with you on the road by sundown tomorrow," said Scott.

"It will be easy for me. Even a niño can follow these wagon tracks," laughed Miguel. "Adios, mi compadre."

"Adios," laughed Scott.

It took Scott until early afternoon to reach the telegraph lines. Glenrock had a telegraph office, but sending a message from there was out of the question. Riding cross-country doubled his traveling time, but Scott felt it was worth it. The unexpected small things always caused you trouble in one of these covert operations. He couldn't really just climb any telegraph pole. A stray cowhand seeing him climbing a pole and tapping into the telegraph line would soon be the talk of every local saloon for miles around. Scott followed the line until it veered away from what looked like a main road. A short rope throw and a little pressure from his horse pulled one of the poles down to where he could reach it by standing on some boulders. Once finished, he could just leave the pole leaning, a common enough occurrence, and wouldn't require any repairs since he would leave the wire intact. Using a small Army field telegraph key, Scott sent:

Have found some nuggets STOP
Following trail to mother lode STOP
Claim probably between Silver Creek and
Glenrock STOP
Claim still secret STOP
WS

This message wouldn't mean much to anyone that might receive it, but when it was ultimately relayed to Washington, the Chief would understand. Scott had asked the next operator to forward the message to the Army post in Denver, and with the alternate coded address, he knew the message would be on the Chief's desk by morning. If they needed to relay information, it would be left at the telegraph offices in both Silver Creek and Glenrock. Unfortunately, Scott didn't think they would be able to retrieve any return messages.

Scott rode for an hour before making camp at a small spring he had located using the Army survey maps he had picked up in Pittsville, maps the Chief had arranged to be left there by an Army courier. He built a small fire and chewed on the rest of the jerky from his saddlebags and drank clear spring water. His mind drifted to thoughts of the family horse farm and his brother's daughters, 15 and 17. Only lately had he begun to think nostalgically about his family and his own lack of roots. It wasn't so much real thoughts, as it was a deep-down feeling that wasn't fully formed. The feelings didn't keep him awake for long as he drifted into a deep sleep, only to be disturbed by his horse's occasional snort and foot stomp.

Scott was up and riding shortly after sunup. He wanted to rendezvous before nightfall with Miguel. He stopped around midday by a stream. There he ate some more beef jerky and hard tack. He treated himself to a tin of peaches from his saddlebags and knew from his maps that he would easily make the rendezvous.

CHAPTER 13

Eddie was stepping off the train in New Haven, the home of Princeton University, by 3:00 p.m. Having never been there, Eddie asked the conductor for directions.

Eddie pushed open the door of the police station and hesitated. There was a sergeant sitting at a raised desk just like the stations in New York City.

"Can we help you, mister?" asked the sergeant.

"I hope so. My name is Eddie Donnally. I'm from the Treasury Department in Washington, and I would like to speak with the Chief." Eddie displayed his commission book to the sergeant, who quickly replied, "Wait here. Let me check when he can see you."

Before Eddie could take a seat, the sergeant returned. "He said to bring you right in." The sergeant took Eddie down a short hall to a closed door marked Chief. The sergeant gave a rap, opened the door for Eddie, and once Eddie was inside, he shut the door.

"Welcome to New Haven, Mr. Donnally," greeted the Chief, whose desk plate read Martin Flaherty. "Hey, you look familiar," he exclaimed. "You any relation to John O'Hara in the New York Police Department?"

Eddie smiled, "He's my uncle on my mother's side and people have been saying we look alike for years. Are you retired from New York?" asked Eddie.

"Yeah, I came out here several years back so my wife could

care for her elderly mother. Plus the city made the school waive the tuition for my kid," answered the Chief. "Have a seat, son."

The Chief stepped to a sideboard and took out a bottle of Irish whiskey and two glasses. After pouring two shots, the Chief toasted, "Here's to your health," and they both threw back the shot.

"Okay, let's get down to business," said Chief Flaherty. "I know you're not here for your health."

"I'm trying to track down any information I can about a student at the university about 18 years ago," said Eddie.

"Jeez," exclaimed the Chief. "That's a long time ago. But you are in luck. Kevin O'Connell was the chief back then and he is still around. He is old-fashioned, though; doesn't have anything much to do with anybody that's not Irish. I'm glad you're the one that showed up. Kevin is tight-lipped, too, and since you haven't mentioned a name, it must be sensitive," said Chief Flaherty.

"You can't even imagine," said Eddie.

In 30 minutes, Eddie was sitting in the small house of Kevin O'Connell. The house was neat as could be and had an obvious woman's touch. Eddie assumed Mrs. O'Connell was out. After another hospitable round of Irish whiskey, Kevin O'Connell said, "Okay, what can I do for a fellow Irishman?"

"Hold your horses, Kevin. I know this is something sensitive, so I'm going back to the station. I'm not sure I want to know. I'll take the carriage back and turn him around. He'll be waiting for you when you're ready to go, Eddie," advised Chief Flaherty. "See you, Kevin," he hollered as he went out the door.

Kevin looked at Eddie expectantly. "Don't worry, my wife is down at the church. She won't be back until later."

"The person I'm interested in is Alvin T. Maddox, the current Secretary of the Treasury," replied Eddie.

Kevin O'Connell burst out laughing. "I've been waiting for somebody to try to put that no-count in jail for years. I've got a whole file from back then. Be right back."

Eddie was too stunned to speak. When the older man returned, he had an obviously neat file.

"Everything you need is in here," said Kevin. "Take a quick look and see if you have any questions while I make a spot of tea."

The file was neatly handwritten and was totally legible even though it was nearly 20 years old. It detailed how Andrew White, the Secretary's cousin, had his hand in all kinds of crime. Kevin's report went on to say that he believed Maddox to be the brains behind White. The file also mentioned a student named Stang, who was described as a close associate of White and Maddox. The report concluded that Stang was more of an errand boy without any real guts.

As Kevin returned with a tray, he asked Eddie, "You get to the part about Stang, now the Secretary of the Interior?"

"This is so much more than I expected," exclaimed Eddie.

"The bad news is, I was never able to get enough hard evidence to charge any of them. The group moved on as soon as Maddox and Stang graduated. White might have spent one term at the university, but that was it. White and a local Italian kid, named what else, Guido, did a lot of strong arm stuff. I don't have to tell you how difficult it is to charge kids with money," apologized the former Chief.

As they sipped tea, Eddie's mind was racing.

"I can see those wheels turning in your head, young man. I

wouldn't give that stuff to anyone but another mick. Nobody else has enough sense to catch them," said Kevin laughing. "You can take it with you. That bunch will never be coming back here. Don't underestimate them, though. You know the Italian kid, we found him floating in the river two weeks after the others supposedly left town."

"You don't know the value of this file," announced Eddie.

"I like speaking with you young guys, but I suspect you are itching to get back to D.C. There is a late train, so you need to get going if you expect to be on it," advised the older man.

They both stood up and shook hands. "One thing, son, if you get them, you got to come back and tell me all about it. Be sure to come with a good bottle of Irish whiskey, too," laughed the former Chief, ushering Eddie out the door.

The old man went back to the table and poured himself a half glass of Irish whiskey. Holding it up to the light, he said to himself, "Now this is what I call a good day."

The carriage was waiting as the Chief had promised, and Eddie went straight to the train station. To the policeman driving the carriage, Eddie said, "Apologize to your chief for my bad manners at rushing out of town. Tell him I owe him one. He'll understand."

Eddie was ecstatic. He would be in the Chief's office first thing tomorrow morning. He had expected it to take several days making very discreet indirect inquiries. Thank God for Irishmen, thought Eddie, and crossed himself.

CHAPTER 14

While Eddie was off to New Haven, Operative John Bell went to a blue collar neighborhood not too far from the BEP building. The area was full of boarding houses and houses with rooms to let. John went to an address and knocked.

A heavyset woman with gray hair answered the door.

"Would you be Mrs. Jackson?" asked Bell, getting the woman's name from a plate beside the front door.

"That would be me," she answered noncommittally.

Bell went to pull out his badge and commission book.

"Get in here," she hissed. "Anybody sees a badge and I won't get another renter for a month. I knew you was a copper, soon as you came up the walk."

Bell followed the landlady into a sitting parlor and took the offered seat.

"Who is it this time:" she asked warily.

"I know some other officers were around, but I'd like to hear about the two brothers," apologized Bell.

"What's to tell?" spat the woman. "They just up and left. At least their monthly rent was paid up."

The landlady gave Bell a good description of the brothers and remarked on their understanding and speaking English, even though they spoke with distinctive German accents.

"Did anybody see them leave, Mrs. Jackson?" asked Bell.

"No, nobody was around. One of the neighbors said she saw them leaving with two guys, but she only saw them from the back. She did say one of them had long silver hair like one of those politicians," answered the landlady.

"I think that's all I need," said Bell. "Thanks for your help."

"I liked those boys, and they paid their rent on time and were clean. I wish I had a whole house full of them," she replied as she showed Bell to the door.

"If you can find out anything else, please get in touch," said Bell, handing her his card. "I gather coppers are not real welcome around here."

The landlady just smiled.

CHAPTER 15

John Bell and Eddie Donnally arrived in the lobby of their building at the same time.

"Hey, Eddie, I thought you would be gone a few days," said Bell.

"So did I," replied Eddie. "But I got real lucky up there."

"Yeah, yeah, I know," said Bell, "Luck of the Irish. When are you going to fill me in?"

"Let's go straight to the Chief's office," said Eddie.

Eddie had picked Bell to do the interview regarding the BEP employees because he knew him to be a detail fanatic. While he trusted all the guys in the office, Eddie knew that once Bell was asked not to discuss the case with anyone, that was the way it would be.

"Morning Doris," said Eddie, giving the Chief's secretary a big smile.

"Save that blarney for somebody else," she snapped. "He's not here yet and there has already been a telegram put on his desk."

"We'll just wait," said Eddie.

It wasn't 15 minutes until the Chief came bustling into the office.

"Donnally, what the heck are you doing here?" barked the Chief. "Get in here, you two. Doris, why don't you go get a cup of coffee and visit the girls down in the steno pool?" the Chief instructed.

"There's a telegram on your desk, and I'll be back when I'm good and ready," she snapped, knowing the Chief was clearing her out of the office.

"Believe me, Doris, you don't want to know," apologized the Chief.

Once in the Chief's office, the two operatives sat and waited while the Chief read the telegram.

"Good news," said the Chief. "Will and Miguel have found some evidence and are close to locating the plant. Maybe I was all wrong about the other things."

John Bell, not knowing the entire story, was looking at both men, wondering what was happening.

"Unfortunately, Chief, what I found up in New Haven confirms all your suspicion," informed Eddie.

The Chief stood and took the envelope containing the counterfeit and the genuine currency and handed it to Eddie. "Go ahead and brief John. I'm going to go for a walk and try to clear my head so we can get a plan going."

The Chief was back in 15 minutes and settled in his desk chair. "All right, let's have it and see where we go from here," he ordered.

"I'll go first," said Eddie. "I got to New Haven and was extremely lucky. The Chief of Police is retired from New York City and knew my uncle. The Secretary's time there was long before him, but the previous Chief is a crusty old Irishman named Kevin O'Connell. Not only did he remember the Secretary, he had a whole file with associates, descriptions, everything, which is all in this file he gave me," said Eddie, holding up the file. "O'Connell said the bunch was into all kinds of things. Protection, loan sharking, gambling, you name it. The main guy was Andrew White, the Secretary's cousin. Once the Secretary graduated, the whole bunch left town. O'Connell always believed Maddox was the brains, with White and an Italian kid named Guido providing the muscle."

"Just those three?" asked the Chief.

"No, our other favorite politician, Secretary Stang was part of it, but O'Connell thought he was always just an errand boy. I think O'Connell will go to his grave wishing he would have got them, but he just couldn't get the evidence," added Eddie.

Seeing the concerned look on Eddie's face, the Chief sighed. "Let's hear the rest."

"About two weeks after the bunch left town, the Italian kid, Guido, was found floating in the river," said Eddie.

Turning toward Bell, the Chief asked, "Anything on the brothers?"

"I think so," said Bell. "The landlady gave me a description of two men the neighbors said left with our two."

"One of them roughly fits the description of Andrew White," Eddie said. "O'Connell described him as having prematurely gray hair that he always wore long. The neighbor described one of them as having long silver hair like a politician."

"This is great," said the Chief, rubbing his temples. We've got two prominent politicians here in D.C. probably involved. Will and Miguel are following what they believe will lead to the printing plant out West. The people out West are probably extremely dangerous, and we have no idea how it all fits together. On top of that, we've got no way to reach Will until we hear from him again."

"That about sums it up," said Eddie glumly.

"Well, I'm not willing to live with that. We're going to at least try something," declared the Chief. "Eddie, does the BEP still photograph all their employees?"

"Yeah, they do Chief," answered Eddie.

"Those two brothers have the kind of skill it takes to make this quality of counterfeit. Do you have anybody that could get us photos of those two brothers?" asked the Chief.

Eddie paused. "I believe I do, but it will cost us a bottle of Irish whiskey. He won't say a word, because I know where he goes sometimes on Saturday night, and he is deathly afraid of his wife."

"Just get the photos and beat the bushes down at Union Station. I know it's been a good while, but let's try and see if we can find somebody that remembers them," continued the Chief. "John, you start shadowing Secretary Stang. I'd like to say take more of the men, but we just can't. I know you can't stay with him all the time, but let's just see what some of his patterns are," ordered the Chief.

"I'll get right on him, Chief," said Bell. "Since he was the errand boy before, maybe he still is. Maddox will try to keep his distance."

"I'll try to see what Maddox is doing. I can't be too friendly with him since I can't stand the little weasel and have always avoided being around him when I could," advised the Chief. "So we're clear on what everybody's doing?" asked the Chief.

Donnally and Bell both nodded.

"All right then. Don't write anything down, and keep me posted every morning," said the Chief, waving them out of his office.

When Doris came back in a few minutes, the Chief went out and sat down next to her desk.

Doris arched one eyebrow. "What is it you want?" she asked.

"Am I that easy to read?" asked the Chief.

"You men are always easy to read," she declared.

"Are you friendly with the lady who works for The Secretary, what's her name, Audrey?" asked the Chief.

"You know I am," answered Doris, "And you know we go to lunch occasionally."

"Do you think you could meet her soon and maybe find out what his highness's schedule is like the next few weeks?" the Chief pleaded.

"I assume you want me to do this without making her suspicious," stated Doris.

"That would be nice," said the Chief.

"I'll get right on it," Doris answered. "And, by the way, I'm darn sure I don't want to know anything about this."

The Chief got up and went in his office. In all the time Doris had worked for him, it was the first time he could ever remember her even come close to swearing!

CHAPTER 16

As they left the Chief's office, John Bell turned to Eddie. "I'm going on over to the Interior Department's offices and see if I can pick him up at lunch time. I want to get a good look at him and get a feel for how he acts," Bell said.

"I'll meet you tomorrow morning at the Chief's office," said Eddie. Eddie knew that John Bell was truly a shadow. He was the best operative in the office when it came to surveillance.

Eddie went straight to the BEP and found a park bench near the employees' entrance. He knew his target, Jimmy Anderson, went to lunch at a small Irish pub a few blocks away. Eddie didn't want to go in the building. There were too many people who knew him in there. The Secret Service had arrested BEP employees in the past, and Eddie wanted no attention drawn to himself.

At the stroke of noon, Jimmy came out and made the left toward the pub. Eddie was walking beside him within half a block. "Top of the morning, Jimmy," said Eddie.

Anderson jumped. "Sweet Mary. Where the heck did you come from?" asked the startled man.

Anderson was a middle-aged clerk with the personnel department of the BEP and had been there for years.

"I need a little favor, Jimmy," said Eddie.

"What else is new?" asked Jimmy, rolling his eyes. Jimmy Anderson would occasionally sneak off and visit the Johnson Boarding House, which only had women tenants. Eddie had found it out during an investigation at the BEP and let Anderson know he was doing him a favor by keeping it to himself. Through Anderson, Eddie could get information about any BEP employee without raising any suspicions. "You remember the Hamptman brothers who worked at the BEP?" asked Eddie.

"Of course I do, "snapped Jimmy. "They skipped town just before being arrested. It's no wonder. Everybody in the building knew they were about to get pinched."

"I need their photographs right away, and I mean no one needs to know except me and you," said Eddie, giving Anderson a hard look.

"Okay," Jimmy said. "Give me a couple of days."

"What didn't you understand, Jimmy?" asked Eddie. "I need those pictures when you come out this evening."

"Please, Eddie," pleaded Jimmy. "Somebody might notice."

"It's your job to make sure no one notices, and I mean you tell no one," glared Eddie. "I'm not going to even bother threatening you."

"I'll do my best," weaseled Jimmy Anderson.

"Now, that's the right attitude," said Eddie. "I'll meet you around here at quitting time."

As Jimmy Anderson turned into his favorite lunch spot, Eddie just kept walking.

CHAPTER 17

The next morning, Eddie and John Bell were comparing notes with the Chief. Eddie said, "Here are the pictures of the brothers. I got them, and it didn't even cost me any whiskey."

"I watched Stang from lunch until he went home. He looked like he was lunching with some kind of businessmen. They picked up the tab," laughed Bell. "It was lights out at his place around 9 p.m. I hung around just to see if he was coming back out, but nothing."

The Chief sat forward, looking at the pictures of the two brothers. "Good job, both of you," he said. "Let's just keep going. Doris is having lunch with Secretary Maddox's secretary today, and five bucks says we'll know his full schedule by early afternoon. Any takers?" asked the Chief.

"You must be joking," Eddie and Bell answered almost in unison.

"Doris could make the Washington Monument talk," added Eddie.

"She doesn't know anything about the case and doesn't want to," laughed the Chief. "So, I'll see you men again in the morning," added the Chief as Donnally and Bell got up to leave.

Neither man looked at Doris on their way past her desk.

Eddie Donnally agreed with the Chief, but Union Station in Washington was huge. Since the counterfeit money had showed up out West and Will seemed to be hot on the trail, he concentrated on the portion of the station that handled the west-bound trains. Eddie asked for the ticket supervisor and was ushered into a small office behind and around the corner from the ticket stations. "What can I do for you?" asked an older man with glasses and gray hair. The nameplate on his desk read Gerald Greene.

Eddie showed his identification and said, "To be truthful, I'm looking for a needle in a haystack. These are pictures of two brothers I'm trying to track. They are actually Swiss, but have a distinct German accent."

"That may not be such a problem. The ticket window people have amazing memories for faces," said Gerald.

"We think they left town a little over a month ago," said Eddie with a grimace.

"Oh," Gerald said with his eyes widening. "Well, let's go ask anyway. You never can tell. Several of them have gotten rewards for noticing people from the wanted posters we keep in back."

Will showed the pictures to at least 20 ticket sellers with no luck.

"You need to come back after four to catch the night shift," advised Gerald.

"Will you be here?" asked Eddie.

"I'm here until five, so I can take you around," said Gerald. "I have an assistant who does the night shift, but I usually stay over a little while."

"Great," said Eddie. "I'll be back before five." Eddie casually strolled back to the atrium, and to his surprise, he saw a face he recognized. Casually walking up behind the man, Eddie cried, "Boo!"

The startled man jumped and wheeled around.

"Lordy, Mr. Donnally, you almost made me pee myself," squealed Pinky McFadden. "Are you and Mr. Scott out to get me or something?"

"No, but this might be your lucky day again," advised Eddie. He showed Pinky the two pictures. "I'm trying to find anybody who might have seen these two brothers."

"They look foreign," said Pinky.

"They are," replied Eddie. "They're Swiss but speak with a German accent. I'll give you a hundred dollars, and anybody you find that has seen them and can give me some information a hundred dollars."

"Great, I got lots of friends that work around here. This is a sure bet," boasted Pinky. "How did you know I was here, Mr. Donnally?" asked Pinky. "Never mind," he said, shrinking back from Eddie's dirty look.

"Don't lose those pictures. I'll be back here around five o'clock," growled Eddie. "Oh, Pinky, by the way, those two came through here about a month ago," said Eddie, laughing to himself as he turned away from a crestfallen Pinky.

When Eddie got back to Union Station, he was shocked to see Pinky McFadden with another small man in tow.

"Mr. Donnally, this is Wormy," said Pinky.

"Pleased to meet you, Wormy. Do we have something?" asked Eddie.

Wormy removed his hat and said, "I believe I do, sir!"

With an encouraging nudge from Pinky, he continued. "About a month ago, those two gents in the pictures were here in the station waiting for a train going West. I'm not sure which train they took. Anyway, these two looked like foreigners and them foreigners, you know are usually easy pickings." Wormy was rocking from foot to foot.

"Okay," said Eddie. "Keep going."

"Well, as I moved into position and started to get close, I spotted another guy with them. He wasn't real big, but he was kinda mean looking and he was watching those two like they were prisoners or something. They were joined by another guy who was white haired and had their tickets. I remembered him good because he was wearing a beautiful pair of black cowboy boots. That's not something we see everyday around here. Anyway, I moved on. I didn't want no part of them guys," finished Wormy.

"Pinky, I swear you have the luck of the Irish," said Eddie, as he pulled two one-hundred dollar bills from his jacket pocket and gave each of the men a bill.

Pinky held his bill up to the light and said, "This is not queer or nothing, is it, Mr. Donnally?"

Eddie gave Pinky a withering look. Pinky and Wormy quickly walked away without looking back.

CHAPTER 18

The next morning, the Chief and John Bell were already in the Chief's office when Eddie strolled in. Doris was nowhere to be seen.

"Nothing's happening with that weasel Stang," informed the Chief.

"I've got a little something," said Eddie, laying the pictures out. "I found a dipper at Union Station who remembered these two. He thought they were going to be easy marks, but he noticed a tough guy, sort of, standing watch over them. He didn't remember much about him, but there was another man with them. He was a tall man with white hair and he was wearing a pair of beautiful black cowboy boots."

"Excellent," exclaimed the Chief. "That description is enough to convince me it was Andrew White."

"I also have some investigative news. Doris had lunch with Secretary Maddox's secretary and found out something interesting. It seems the Secretary is going out to Colorado for a celebration in two weeks, and Secretary Stang is going with him!" remarked the Chief.

"What kind of celebration?" Bell and Eddie asked simultaneously.

"It seems the BEP is shipping 20 million dollars out to a place called Silver Creek and bringing back 20 million in gold," answered the Chief. "I spoke to the BEP Chief last night, and he graciously invited me along. He knows how much I like the

West."

"Are we going with you?" asked Eddie. "Silver Creek is one of the places Will mentioned in his telegram."

"Listen, I'd like to take you and some of the other guys, but we can't take the chance," apologized the Chief. "Besides, we really have no idea what this bunch is up to. It would be like them to be out of town and the actual crime take place here. So, we are all going to go about our business as usual."

"I know I'm speaking for John, too, Chief, when I tell you to be careful," said Eddie. "I got to say, this is truly a mystery right now. Maybe we will hear something from Will soon."

"I hope so," echoed the Chief.

On the way out, Eddie gave Doris a wink, and was rewarded with a slight upturn of her lips.

When they got back to their office, John stopped Eddie just outside the door.

"I'll just keep an eye on Stang for awhile," said Bell.

"Good idea, John. They have to be communicating somehow," said Eddie.

Both men entered the office like it was just another day on the job.

CHAPTER 19

It was mid-afternoon when Will noticed the dark spots against the sky, but it didn't really worry him. Vultures were a common sight circling over some animal that was dying or had recently died. An hour later, he realized they were circling generally over the area where he was headed. He intersected the main road between Glenrock and Silver Creek, edged his horse into a ground eating lope and tried to quiet his growing apprehension. He rounded a bend in the road and saw the mule's carcass lying across the trail in front of him. He drove his horse forward, even though it tried to shy away from the dead smell.

Scott could see that the mule had taken a load of buckshot from close range right in the head and neck. There was blood everywhere, but no Miguel. Scott rode his horse back down the trail and tied him to a tree. He then walked up, trying to figure out what happened. He circled the area and quickly recognized the ambush plan.

One man, wearing big boots had crouched down behind some boulders next to the trail and probably fired the shotgun. The other man had hidden up the trail a little and Scott counted four spent rifle cartridges in the dirt, which he retrieved. He quickly circled the dead mule and picked up the running tracks of Miguel's horse as it fled back down the trail away from the ambush. It wasn't 20 feet before he saw a splash of blood.

Scott ran to his horse and quickly began tracking the fleeing horse's path back down the trail. The terrified horse had run at least two miles before slowing. Every so often, there were large splashes of blood and Scott could tell that eventually the horse was simply wandering down the trail with no direction from his rider. He almost missed the side trail that cut off the main road. In fact, if he hadn't been so closely watching the horse tracks, he would have missed it. The trail was not hidden, but it blended so well with the background rocks and trees that it was barely noticeable, but Miguel's horse had obviously come this way. He knew the horse's tracks and he saw a splash of blood on the leaves of a small aspen he had to brush past. The trail, though obscure, was obviously well used and wide enough for a wagon. Scott noticed that someone had pulled several fallen logs away from the trail to keep it clear. The trail skirted around a tree and Scott kneed his horse forward, into what seemed like a pass between two small hills. There were wagon tracks, but not those of a heavy freight wagon. The trail led through a small aspen grove next to a tumbling mountain stream, which Scott barely noticed as he drove his horse at a canter toward a log cabin nestled against the side of a towering butte. As Scott reined his horse to a stop in front of the cabin, he heard the lever actions of several Winchesters being worked. "I'm not here for any kind of trouble, but I tracked my best friend's horse to here and I just know he's hurt bad," panted Scott, trying to control his emotions.

"Shuck that gun, mister, and step down," came a voice from Scott's right. The voice belonged to a young man holding a rifle that made him in charge at any age. He was behind the corner of the porch next to the house.

Scott unbuckled his gun belt, looped it around the saddle

horn and swung out of the saddle. The front door opened further and another young man with a rifle motioned for Scott to come inside. Scott strode up the steps and followed the man through a living room and into a large bedroom.

Miguel was lying in a large four poster bed, his right side swathed in bandages. As Scott moved closer, he could see Miguel was pale and his breathing shallow.

"How bad is he?" asked Scott to no one in particular.

"It's too soon to tell," replied a female, who Scott hadn't noticed. "He's got two bullet holes in his back and some minor buckshot wounds to his legs."

Scott turned to face the voice and was stunned speechless by the beauty of the dark-haired woman facing him. She was dressed in a crisp white shirt and wearing Levi's, like a man with knee high riding boots. It was the last thing he expected.

"We were able to get the bullets out, but he had lost a lot of blood before he got here," said the lady. "We don't get too many strangers visiting here. It's not easy unless you know we're here."

The question was there, even though not specifically asked: Who are you and what is this all about?

"My name is Will Scott, and this is Miguel Fernandez, my partner," replied Scott, trying to gather his thoughts. "We've got a small claim in these parts and I had some business to take care of in town, so Miguel came on ahead. I found our pack mule dead on the main road and I followed Miguel's tracks back to here."

"Let's go to the kitchen and let him sleep," instructed the woman.

Scott followed her down the hall, noticing for the first time the size of the house and the quality of its furnishings. What he had first thought was a log cabin was not that at all. The log front with the porch was the center of the house, but off to each side were additional rooms, each curved with windows facing out on the valley. It was unusual architecture for the West, yet it effectively matched the site on which the house was built.

They entered a large kitchen, and Scott sat down at the square table in the center of the room.

"My name is Lisa Butler. This is the Cataloochee Ranch. It belongs to me and my two brothers, Albert and Carl, as well as Uncle Frank," said the woman, who appeared to be in her late 20's. As if on cue, two medium-sized men walked through the door and placed their Winchesters in a corner gun rack. Albert was obviously several years older than Lisa, while Carl looked to be about 21. Both men looked like they were outdoorsmen, but neither had the look of a seasoned western rancher that spent days and days in the sun and weather.

"Don't forget me," boomed a voice behind Scott. An older man stomped into the room and offered his hand to Scott.

"Who could ever forget you, Uncle Frank?" beamed Lisa.

"Frank Schuster, mister. I am the foreman here when I'm not too busy doing something else," growled the older man.

The three of them broke into an easy laugh at the older man.

"I'm Will Scott and my partner is Miguel Fernandez. I was supposed to meet up with him by this evening, but it looks like some claim jumpers had other plans," advised Scott.

"I'm taking this broth to Miguel; that is, if I can get him to wake up enough to take some. There's coffee here, so you boys help yourselves," said Lisa, leaving with a laden tray.

"Your friend's pretty lucky, mister. If he hadn't ended up

here, he'd be dead by now." said Schuster. "Lisa will pull him through, if anybody can. She seems to have the healing touch. Her whole life, she's healed anything that's gotten sick around here—animals, people, plants. Yes sir, he's real lucky."

"I'll go out and take care of your horse and store your gear in the guest room," spoke up Carl. "We don't have a bunk house."

"I'll go with you," said Scott. "There's not much I can do here."

The two men walked outside to Scott's horse and led him around the side of the house to the nearby barn. Scott marveled to himself at the sheer natural beauty of the place and the way the buildings blended with the natural surroundings.

"This is some fine horse you have here, Mr. Scott," said Carl.

"Call me Will, and yes, he is," said Scott." We just bought these from a gypsy fella over by Central City, when we cashed our dust."

"Was Miguel's horse injured?" asked Scott.

"No, just winded and spooked by the blood and everything when he got here," said Carl, swinging open the barn door.

Scott led his horse into a barn unlike most others in the West. This was no ramshackle outbuilding built with leftovers. It was as solid as the house and had a wood floor, something unheard of in the West. He led his horse into a stall and stripped off the saddle.

"This is some barn, Carl. I can't recall seeing another one just like it," said Scott.

"There's not another one like it this side of the Mississippi," said Carl. "It's patterned after barns my mother knew back in New England."

"Your mother must be quite a lady," said Scott.

"She died a couple of years ago," said Carl, taking Scott's saddle and placing it next to Miguel's on a nearby saddle rack. "But you're right, she was a special kind of person."

They fed and watered Scott's horse and Miguel's before walking out of the barn. Scott noticed a small corral off the barn which contained eight or ten high quality horses.

"You have some fine horses there yourself," said Scott, admiring the gaits of the horses as they paced around.

"My sister specializes in horses, while the rest of us are concerned with the cattle," replied Carl.

"How many head do you run here?" asked Scott.

"We have 1000 head of what most people call breeder cattle," said Carl. "It is a cross of Hereford to Red Angus. Grows twice as fast as most breeds, and they are really bout the hardiest cattle around. People buy them to improve their cattle herds, so we get top dollar."

"It doesn't take nearly as many head to turn a profit," Scott said, shocked. "How much land do you have here? I didn't know you could run that many cattle in this part of Colorado."

"This valley is special. We have all the water we need and the grass grows knee high most everywhere," said Carl, not really answering the question about the size of the ranch.

As they walked in the back door of the house, Lisa was soaking bandages in a strong-smelling antiseptic on the kitchen table.

"I am glad you're back," she said, looking at Will. "You can help me change your partner's bandages. Wash your hands and arms in the sink there and we'll do some doctoring. I got some broth in him, but he didn't really wake up. It was just reflex."

Scott did as he was told and followed her to the bedroom with a tray full of the strong-smelling bandages. He couldn't help but notice Lisa's trim figure and gentle sway as he followed her.

Miguel's condition was unchanged. Scott could see the beads of sweat on Miguel's brow and knew the fever was starting. Lisa quickly stripped off the old bandages, being careful not to start any fresh bleeding.

"Just take some of these bandages and press them gently against the wounds," she instructed. "The poultice will help draw out the infection."

Scott again did as he was told and noticed that every so often Miguel would wince at the gentle pressure they were applying.

"I don't really believe we are hurting him any," said Lisa, noticing Will's own grimace.

Scott nodded and said nothing. The lump in his throat prevented words. Scott's hands began to tremble as his emotions reeled. He felt relief at finding Miguel, remorse and guilt for being the cause of this.

Lisa gently guided him to an armchair where he sat dumbly watching her finish what they had started.

"I don't know how long this fever is going to last, but if he can live through this, he'll make it. You stay with him for now and I'll come back later. My room is across the hall, so just yell if you need help!" explained Lisa.

"Thanks a lot," said Will weakly.

"You're obviously very close. I hope he makes it for your sake," she said, giving his hand a gentle squeeze as she left the room.

Scott settled into the chair and dozed off and on the rest of the night. Every so often, Miguel would say a few words in Spanish, but even though Scott could understand it, the words didn't really mean anything. All Scott could do was apply cool cloths to his injured friend's forehead and hope.

It was just before dawn that Lisa's gentle shaking roused him.

"Come on and get some sleep. His fever seems a little better now," she said, taking Scott's arm and leading him across the hall to her room. She sat him down on the bed and the last thing he remembered was the white canopy over the bed.

CHAPTER 20

Sunlight was streaming in when Scott woke up. He lay still trying to get his mind and surroundings together. His eyes settled on the clean clothes lying on a nearby chair and realized they were from his saddlebags. He also realized he was wearing nothing but his underwear.

Suddenly, the door opened and Lisa tiptoed in with a tray holding a pot of coffee and two cups.

"How's Miguel?" Scott asked.

A startled Lisa yelped and almost dropped the tray. Scott started to get out of the bed and help, but remembering his state of undress, he quickly changed his mind.

"There's good news! Miguel's fever broke shortly after dawn. He was awake and I gave him some broth. I told him you were here and he seemed relieved."

"I've got to talk to him," said Scott.

"He's asleep again and believe me, he's not going anywhere," she replied.

"How is he really?" asked Scott.

"I think he'll be fine with several weeks of rest. One of you two must be living right, 'cause by all rights, he should be dead," she answered with a questioning look.

"I would really like to do something to repay you for what you've done," said Scott, trying to change the subject, knowing that his impromptu story about claim jumpers would not stand up to close scrutiny, especially since the ambush had been on a main road between two towns. "I'll tell you what. If you think you can keep up, you can ride with me down the valley to check on my horses," she said. "Your friend is going to sleep a lot and our housekeeper, Louisa, will look after him now."

"I'd like to but I need to go get our mining stuff off our dead mule," said Will.

"Don't worry about that. Carl is up there now getting your stuff," replied Lisa. "He gets bored sometimes and looks for an adventure."

"That's not much of an adventure, stripping a dead mule," answered Scott.

"We don't get a lot of excitement around here," she replied, laughing.

"I'll get dressed and meet you in the kitchen," said Scott.

"Lisa started to walk out carrying a cup of the coffee and just as she got to the door, she said, "You needn't be so embarrassed. How do you think you got that way?" She closed the door behind her with a slight laugh. Men are so easy, she thought. I've got two brothers. I'm not going to undress a total stranger!

Will Scott was struck speechless, and then couldn't decide which was hotter, the burning of his face or the hot coffee she had left behind.

When Scott got to the kitchen, Lisa was talking to a middle-aged Mexican woman who was tending to some type of wonderful smelling stew.

"Louisa, this is Mr. Will Scott. He's prospecting for another Comstock Lode," she said.

"Buenos días, senor, I will take good care of your friend," Louisa replied.

"Thank you very much," replied Scott, "And God knows, you've been doing good so far."

"Let's do some real work, Mr. Miner," said Lisa, picking up a saddle bag from the table and heading for the door.

When they got to the barn, the horses were saddled and ready to ride. Scott's rifle scabbard, holstered handgun and saddle bags were leaning against the saddle rack. His horse was standing next to a beautiful filly that whinnied as she saw Lisa walk up.

"Hello, baby," said Lisa, giving the horse's velvet nose a quick rub.

"She's a beautiful horse," said Scott, admiring both the owner and the horse.

"She is, but that's a fine horse she's standing beside," said Lisa, swinging into the saddle. "What's his name?"

"Yeah, we were lucky to get these horses," said Scott, fighting the urge to brag. "His name is Animoso."

They cantered out of the yard and followed a small stream that spread out when it reached the bottom of the hill. The trail was flat and showed a lot of horse prints. The floor of the valley was covered in lush green grass that reached up to where the trees started.

"I don't think I've ever seen a more beautiful valley," said Scott, taken by the sheer natural beauty of the valley. "You must have a lot of water here."

"My father and mother both felt the same way," said Lisa.

"How did all this come to be?" asked Scott.

"Well, my father was a geologist, and he came West figuring he could make his fortune mining. He had all the technical skills that the developing mining barons needed to fully develop the claims they were buying from, the striking it rich prospectors. My father struck out on his own and started buying up promising claims and then reselling them to the big syndicates that sold shares to the greedy speculators back East. Most of the claims were decent, so my father made a lot of money, as did the men like Hearst and Tabor. The speculators usually didn't do too well, but people who expect something for nothing usually don't."

"That's an interesting story, but it doesn't explain the house and everything else," mused Scott.

"All right, but it's my family history, so I get to tell it like I want," laughed Lisa. "Anyway, Dad found this area while checking out some claims around here and ultimately bought all the land. At that time, if there wasn't gold or silver on the land, nobody wanted it. Dad was always fascinated by this area. He said it was a freak of nature, that this whole valley had its beginnings thousands of years ago. He found some gullies where there are all kinds of fossils from the oceans buried on the walls. He would sometimes dig up samples and send them back to a friend of his at the University in Boston."

"Where does your mother fit into all of this?" asked Scott.

"You are not content to just let me tell this story, are you? I don't even know you but here I am telling you my whole family history," fumed Lisa.

She urged her horse into a gallop and Scott followed her off the main trail through an aspen grove until she pulled up at a small spring. She swung down off her horse and let her horse take a drink. Scott followed her off his horse and they let the horses graze on the lush grass.

"You ride pretty good for a prospector," she joked.

"I guess I could say you ride pretty good for a lady, but I'm not sure you'd take that as a compliment," he joked back.

"At least you noticed," she said. "My mother is really the reason for the ranch. Dad made his fortune and went back East to take care of the rest of his family. Problem was, the West had gotten into his blood, this valley in particular. My mother was a city girl from Boston, even though her family owned a big farm outside of the city. Her ideas of the West came from dime novels and newspaper stories. But she and my father fell in love and made a deal. They'd come to the valley, but he had to bring New England along." She laughed and continued. "That's why the house and barn and things are built like they are—the New England way. They were really good for each other. I guess that's why Dad didn't live too long after she died. He just kind of up and decided to die. She died about two years ago, and he went six months later. I was in Boston being the social butterfly when she died, and by the time I got back here, there wasn't much left to do but bury my father." She wiped her eyes and exclaimed, "Enough of this mess, I don't know what's got into me. Let's ride!"

They mounted up and spent the next couple of hours counting foals and calves. There was a small but fine herd of horses that was undoubtedly worth a lot of money. The cows were also large and extremely healthy looking.

"How do you round the horses and cattle up? You don't have any hands," asked Scott.

"Once a year we have a roundup and get it all done at once. We put a lot of work into that one month. The men are all vaqueros that come up on a cattle drive from New Mexico. The foreman on a big ranch down there is Louisa's brother. They've been doing it for years, so we all know each other. It's really hard work, but it's really a grand time. You should see the way they ride and work the cows and horses. Come on, I'll race you back to the barn."

Scott urged Animoso forward in an effort to catch up to the girl who was away at full gallop. It was about a mile and a half back to the house and the two horses were side by side most of the way. In the last half mile, Scott's horse pulled ahead, and when they clattered into the yard, Animoso was fifty yards in front.

Carl, Albert and the crusty old foreman met them in the yard, drawn by the pounding hooves and the pair's enthusiastic yelling.

"Congratulations," exclaimed Lisa. "That must be the fastest horse in the state. I didn't think you could outrun Contessa like that."

"Just got lucky, ma'am," beamed Scott, barely suppressing his pride in his horse.

"I'll cool them down," said Carl, taking the reins and leading the horses toward the barn and corral.

"Y'all come inside. Louisa made lemonade and your friend swallowed some broth and was sleeping until you yahoos came flying into the yard," said Albert.

"That was some fine riding, mister," said Schuster, the smile on his face offset by the hard suspicion Scott could see in his eyes. Scott knew his foolish pride in pushing Animoso to outrun Contessa was a mistake.

While the others pulled up chairs in the kitchen, Scott tiptoed down the hall to see Miguel. A weak smile appeared on Miguel's face as Scott slipped into the room.

"Buenas días, Senor Will," said Miguel.

"You had me worried, amigo," breathed Scott, gently grasping his friend's hand.

"They were waiting for us on the trail. One of them was up on the rocks with a rifle, and the other was hiding beside the trail with the shotgun. When the rifle fired, the mule bolted and that is what saved me; the big man stood up and fired, but the mule he was loco and jump in between. The mule, he almost fall on my horse. I remember my horse running and more rifle shots but not much else."

"How did you find me and bring me here?" asked Miguel.

Scott recounted the events of the past two days and said, "You go to sleep and we'll talk more later."

"Señor Will, these are really bad hombres. They knew we were behind them and they mean to kill us for sure," cautioned Miguel.

"I know, we've got some real planning to do when you feel better," replied Scott.

"Buenos noches, mi amigo," sighed Miguel, closing his eyes.

CHAPTER 21

Scott closed the door quietly and eased down the hall back toward the kitchen. Everybody in the room, including the cook Louisa looked up at him as he entered the room. Scott knew without a doubt he had been the topic of their conversation.

Despite their curiosity, the next hour passed by, over lemonade and hot empanadas, without a hitch until the gruff older foreman insisted that evening chores came in front of socializing. Everyone went their separate way, leaving Scott and Lisa alone in the kitchen.

Scott was so relaxed, he almost forgot the counterfeiters and the problems he was facing. So relaxed, he barely comprehended her question.

"How did you and Miguel become partners?" she asked.

"We've been friends a long time. We grew up together and you might say we have been partners since childhood," replied Scott. It wasn't quite the truth, but close, and then, he didn't know exactly why, but he told her the whole story of being in the Army, how he became friends with Jonas and how the black sergeant had saved his life. He felt himself pouring out all the pent-up anger he had felt at the Army for the senseless Indian War that had killed so many of his troops and Indians for no good reason. He saw the tears in her eyes as he recounted the final chapter of his Army career: the raid on the Indian village where the Colonel had ordered everyone—men, women and children—killed. This was a village Scott had scouted and found under the mistaken concept that the natives were being rounded up for relocation to a reservation. While he was talking, her eyes remained locked on his, and to his surprise, he could feel their emotions locked together. "I still have dreams about that day. I guess I should call them nightmares," sighed Will. "But they don't come very often now."

"What happened to the Colonel?" asked Lisa.

"He was transferred out to a northern fort, and that's the last I know," said Will. "I really don't want to know, since I'm not sure I wouldn't kill him if I met him on the street."

"Something tells me you wouldn't do that," said Lisa, with a kind look.

"No, probably not. Jonas and Miguel both offered to go with me to hunt for the low-down murderer. Even though we all will do whatever we need to when it comes to protecting ourselves, cold-blooded murder is what separates us from people like him," declared Will. "You are one of the only people I've ever talked to about that day," added Will, shaking his head.

He found it hard, but he stopped short of telling her about his entry into the Secret Service and the string of successes he had accomplished. Instead, he lied about being a prospector and felt guilty and ashamed while doing it, so guilty, that when Lisa leaned forward and gave him a gentle kiss, not only could he not speak, he didn't move a muscle.

Fortunately for Scott, at that moment Louisa came bursting into the kitchen and the spell was broken. Will stood up and said, "I need to do some work around here to earn our keep. I think I'll go out to the barn and help Carl with the evening chores."

When Will got to the barn, Carl was putting hay in the racks of the stalls where two pregnant mares were waiting expectantly. Will went in and started mucking the stalls, his mind a complete muddle. There were very few people who he had a close connection with, Miguel, his brother, Jonas . . . but he had never felt the close emotional connection he had just experienced with Lisa Butler—never with anyone so fast and never with a woman. Sure, he had been with women; he had even been engaged once, but this had been almost instantaneous and much different. Another disconcerting thing was that despite her kissing him, he knew in his heart that Lisa knew he was not telling her the whole truth.

"Will," called Carl. "Will," he repeated, louder. Will turned with a start. "What are you trying to do, make that stall clean enough for them to eat off the floor?" asked Carl.

"Sorry," said Will, "guess I was just thinking about Miguel."

"They just rang the dinner bell and I'm starving, so let's go get some chow," laughed Carl.

CHAPTER 22

After Scott had left, Lisa stood at the kitchen window and stared down the valley, barely noticing Louisa as she bustled about the kitchen.

"Niña," said Louisa quietly. Lisa turned at the sound of the endearment. "I never see you look at anyone the way you look at this stranger."

Lisa sighed. "I know and it's very unlike me. I barely know this man and yet on the other hand, it seems like I've known him forever. What really scares me is, I know he's not telling me everything. I'm not sure how I know, but I do know."

"The hurt one is like that too. He no say much. He answers a question with a question when he does answer," said Louisa. "He is still hurt bad and will take some time to fully recover, I think."

"I wish those gypsies from last summer were around. Maybe they would tell us the future," said Lisa, and they both laughed. "I'll ring the dinner bell," said Lisa.

Supper passed uneventfully. Scott took a hearty broth up to Miguel, who was able to sit up a little.

"For a man who was shot two days ago, you're doing pretty good," joked Will.

"Please, don't even make me smile," groaned Miguel. "My teeth, they are sore also."

"You'll be better soon," said Will.

"But not soon enough, eh, Capitan?" questioned Miguel.

"No, I guess not. I'm going to wait another day or so and then go try to find those hombres," replied Will. "I don't think they will be watching their back trail as much. They believe you're dead. No one has come looking for either one of us."

"That may be, but those bad men, they know we are after them somehow," said Miguel. "It was an ambush meant for two, not one. Someone here knows about us. The shooting in Leadville, it was no accident. And they surely think I'm dead now. They only have to watch for you."

"You're right, of course. I guess I just didn't want to face it," said Scott resignedly. "I think they also probably know, at least in general terms, what I look like. Someone is feeding them information."

"It's okay, amigo, no man wants to find a rattlesnake in his bedroll," replied Miguel.

"Go to sleep," muttered Scott, picking up the tray and returning to the kitchen.

He quickly washed off the dishes and was able to go to his room without seeing any of the family.

Unfortunately for Will Scott, sleep did not come easily that night. Not only were his personal emotions in an unexpected turmoil, his mind kept going over a plan of action to continue the counterfeit investigation. He really missed talking things out with Miguel. Miguel had natural investigative skills and was very perceptive, but he was in no condition to do anything but concentrate on recovering. Scott had tried to get him to become a full operative with the Secret Service, but Miguel always refused, saying that he felt more comfortable being Will's partner, something that Will really liked. Undercover or covert work was always dangerous, and having someone to cover your actions and help gather information was one of the reasons Will knew the pair had been so successful. Will finally went to sleep knowing that in a day or two at the most, he had to get moving on the trail of the counterfeiters.

CHAPTER 23

The next day Scott and Lisa rode again, but this time Scott rode Miguel's horse, Torreon, just to give the horse some exercise. He was a little skittish at first, since he hadn't been ridden since the ambush. However, after a little while, he settled down and seemed to be enjoying himself. This time they were out almost all day. The horses were more spread out and Lisa was working her horses. She was writing all the foals in a journal with a complete description of both the foal and its mother.

"We sell any of the mares that can't give birth, and I also breed the mares that produce the best foals with Jedidiah Walk, who lives over past Leadville. He's a Quaker man from back East that really knows horses," she explained. "In addition, Don Ramos Gonzalez sends mares up from New Mexico to breed, and he usually wants geldings too. His horses have some old Spanish bloodlines, and he is very careful in his breeding. We have bred some beautiful horses."

"Who breaks and trains them?" asked Will.

"I do the ones we use here on the ranch. Jedediah trains some, but most are trained by the vaqueros down in New Mexico," she answered. "It's about all I can do to breed them and raise them to training age. I try to handle them all from birth and make them people friendly. Even though they run free as a herd, I can walk up to every one of them," she said proudly. They were sitting in the shade at another spring further up the valley, eating the lunches Louisa had packed.

"Why is it that none of what I'm telling you about seems to surprise you?" asked Lisa. "Most men I tell this stuff to tell me it's a bunch of woman's foolishness or just ignore me totally. Horsemen back East have been documenting bloodlines for a long time."

"I don't really know why, but what you're saying seems to make perfect sense to me," lied Scott, looking away and thinking about all the times his grandfather, father and brother had recorded horse bloodlines. He wasn't surprised that a lot of cowboys and ranchers didn't share her views; a lot of them operated on old folk tales when it came to breeding and training horses. When he turned back, her eyes met his and before he realized it, he was kissing her. She returned his kiss with a passion that left them both breathless.

"We better leave or we're going to embarrass these horses," sighed Scott.

"Well, at least you didn't run off this time," said Lisa, laughing at Scott's red face.

"If that's a compliment," said Scott, "then thank you."

They packed up the leftover food and continued their recording work until late afternoon. Once, they saw Albert and Frank on a far ridge doing some cow counting, but neither one returned their waves, as they were intent on their work.

She said, "I want to show you something."

"What?" asked Will.

"Don't worry, you'll be safe," she laughed. "But it is a serious place that I think you will appreciate."

They rode several miles across the valley, which was not real wide at that point, and they came upon a side canyon that was open and flat. Will could see pockets dug out of the canyon walls and some trenches that were just off the edges of the walls. The canyon was not deep and Will could see a small pond up at the end. There was water running, but it disappeared underground about halfway to where they were.

Lisa got off her horse, and Will followed.

"What is this place, some kind of old mining claim?" he asked.

"Not exactly," Lisa replied, walking toward one of the shallow caves dug into the canyon wall.

Will followed, and as they got close, he could see blue veins running in several places across the cave walls.

"Is that turquoise?" Will asked. "I've never seen it in rock like that."

Lisa gave Will a fleeting, funny look, but said, "Dad said Indians have been digging turquoise around here for probably 500 years. You know they call it the sky stone. They believe it connects the earth and the sky and that the turquoise is actually pieces of the sky that have fallen to earth."

"Your dad obviously knew his business," marveled Will.

"Unfortunately, this is a sad place now," said Lisa. "For many years, a small group of Ute Indians, really several families, used to come here in the spring and dig the turquoise. They would take the rough pieces down to New Mexico and trade with the Navajos. When I was growing up, every year after they got here, we would have a big barbecue. Uncle Frank would butcher a cow with several of the Ute Indians. I learned to ride horses bareback holding on to the mane and guiding with my knees." Looking wistful, she continued, "My Dad couldn't stand it that they were digging and chipping using granite and other hard rocks. He got some picks and shovels and brought them out and showed the men and women how to use them. In true Indian fashion, they never took too much of the turquoise, just the amount they thought they would need to trade."

She pointed to another dug out depression in the canyon wall and Will could see picks and shovels lined up against the wall. "They never took the tools with them, just left them here for the next year," she explained.

Will, sensing her despair, took her hand and gently asked, "What happened?"

"When I was 15 or so, we kept waiting for them to come in the spring. We thought they might have been delayed by bad weather up north, but they never came," sighed Lisa. "My mother was beside herself. She had Schuster and some other cowboys ride north, but there was no sign of them. She knew the names of some of the Navajos down in New Mexico, and she, dad and Uncle Frank went down there, but nobody had seen them. Despite all her efforts, she never found them. Every spring for years, we always came out here hoping that they would return."

"I'm sure she tried the Army and the Bureau of Indian Affairs?" questioned Will.

"Of course, but they kept telling her about Comanche raids and how many families died out when they were forced onto the reservations due to smallpox and other illnesses," related Lisa.

"You know I'm so sorry," said Will, "But I know that's not enough."

"It's okay," said Lisa, removing her hand from his. "The

memories are mostly good. It was just a sense of loss for all of us."

Lisa unbuttoned the second button on her shirt and pulled out a heavy silver chain which had a big deep blue turquoise nugget in a beautifully detailed setting.

"The clan leader gave this to my mother one year, and it was the only jewelry we ever saw them have," she related. "My mother treasured it and wore it until the day she died. She insisted I wear it, and I plan to wear it until the day I die. Hopefully, one day I'll have a daughter to pass it on to," she replied, locking eyes with Will.

She turned and mounted up before Will could say anything.

"Your dad never wanted to mine any of the turquoise?" asked Will.

"Not a chance," Lisa said. "Funny, I just got a letter from one of the girls that I went to school with. She lives in New York City. She sent me a newspaper article about Tiffany's, the fancy jewelry company that is selling turquoise jewelry in the city. Uncle Frank says they have a mine down in New Mexico that, like this one, was mined by Indians for hundreds of years."[2]

"The country is getting smaller, I guess," mused Will.

"No one outside of the family knows about this place, and I would suggest you not mention it," growled Lisa. "They might bury you out behind the barn."

The race back to the barn went much the way of the other one—Lisa's mare with early speed, but Torreon just too strong

---

[2] Around 1900, Tiffany's in New York manufactured turquoise jewelry with turquoise originating in the Cerrillos mining district just outside Sante Fe, New Mexico. The original Tiffany Mine is now owned by noted Santa Fe artisan Douglas Magnus. For more information and fascinating history, see www.DouglasMagnus.com

and fast, although the margin of victory was much less.

"Maybe we should mate these two; it seems they might make a good match" said Lisa, once again laughing at Scott's red face. "Too bad yours doesn't have all his parts."

Carl came out from behind the barn and gave Scott a hand with the horses, while Lisa headed to the house.

"That really is a fast horse, too, Will, and strong," said Carl. "Those horses must have cost a lot of money."

"Well, I'm a pretty good bargainer," laughed Will, avoiding a direct answer.

They finished up the horses and headed for the house.

After supper, Miguel was sleeping soundly, so Lisa and Will walked out on the porch and sat in the big rocking chairs, watching the sun settle down over the mountains. Between the setting sun and the panoramic beauty of the valley, a feeling of peacefulness settled over them both. Darkness came with his holding her hand like it was the most natural thing in the world. Unfortunately for them, the entire family slowly migrated to the porch and started discussing their plans for the next day. Eventually the group broke up with everyone, even Scott and Lisa, going to their respective rooms.

CHAPTER 24

With the next day's sunrise, Scott realized he must get moving on the trail of the counterfeiters and made up his mind to tell Lisa he was leaving that night after supper. His big problem was how to get to a telegraph line and notify the Chief of their current circumstances. Before breakfast, he stopped in to see Miguel.

"Buenos días," smiled Miguel at the sight of his friend.

"Good morning, yourself," replied Will. "I'm going to leave in the morning and see if I can pick up the trail of the outlaws."

"Help me sit up, amigo," asked Miguel. Scott did as he was asked, the movement leaving Miguel pale even under his swarthy complexion.

"See, if you wait a few more days, I will be ready to ride after these hombres," stated Miguel.

Scott smiled. "Don't worry so much. You stay here and rest; I won't be gone that long."

"But, they know of us, Señor Will, and there is no help here. Someone in Washington is working against us, no?" asked Miguel.

"I've been doing a lot of figuring over the last couple of days, and it has to be that way. The people out here don't seem to have complete information." stated Scott. "I'm working on a way to smoke them out, but I'm having some trouble figuring out how to work out the details working alone. I will probably telegraph the Chief to see if there are any other operatives anywhere close."

"You are in more trouble than that, Señor Will," laughed Miguel. "I'm stuck in this bed for now, but Louisa has the eyes of the eagle and can keep no secrets. She knows there is something special between you and Lisa. She is constantly asking questions about you, me and your family, and I doubt she believes half of my answers. And you know I am not blind either."

Scott reddened and replied, "I confess that Lisa and this place are special, but these outlaws must be captured and their money destroyed. The other thing, whatever that is, has to wait for now."

Scott eased Miguel back on the bed and left his friend to recover from his brief exertion.

Scott had breakfast with the family and left Lisa going over the ranch's books with Albert while he headed for the barn. Carl was sitting on the porch mending a saddle with a big stitching needle and heavy cord. Scott strolled toward the barn thinking of how to break the news to Lisa that he was leaving for a few days and what story would even be remotely believable. His mind was in a complete turmoil. This case was one of the most important he had ever worked. Not only did he not have a plan for the case, but he had no real idea of what was happening between him and Lisa. What a mess, Scott thought, shaking his head. He walked into the barn heading for his horse's stall and halfway across the wood floor realized he wasn't alone. Scott sensed someone to his right and slowly turned that way, his gun hand sliding toward the gun that wasn't there. Scott recognized Frank Schuster standing in the morning shadows at about the same time he realized he wasn't armed.

"Hello, Frank," said Scott, trying to hide his surprise. Schuster was holding Scott's rifle, a .45 caliber repeater that was the latest in weapons, and the look on his face was definitely not friendly.

"I'm here to have a word with you and get some things straight," said Schuster. "I've been watching you and Lisa, and I can tell she's really taken a shine to you. That in itself is very unusual. There's never been anyone that I've seen her become so attached to, especially almost instantly. Most of the men that have come around here can't hold a candle to her when it comes to riding and handling horses, much less come close to matching her smarts. I don't really understand it, because I've never had it, but Lisa's parents, even though they were totally opposites, had it, and I think you two may have that same feeling in time. But I've also been watching you and listening to the things you say. You know you don't really say too much, mister," and it was clearly a question.

"I guess I'm just not too talkative a fella," shrugged Scott.

"I tell you what you're not, mister, is what you say you are," emphasized Schuster, shifting the rifle a little more forward. "I've watched you ride; you ride as natural as most people walk. Your horse and the Mexican's are probably two of the finest in this part of the country, bar none. They didn't come from some gypsies. You two both have the finest guns money can buy, even though they aren't fancy looking, and there's no doubt they have been fine-tuned by a quality gunsmith. Not only that, I can tell they have been used. I've been around quite a while, you know. I've seen a lot of men who hired their guns out, good ones at it, too. But there haven't been any real gunfighters around for ten to fifteen years, and gunfighter was just a name dreamed up by some dime novelist back East. Most of them were just hired killers, no matter which side of the law they worked on."

"I'm not sure why you're asking me these questions. Most people just kinda mind their own business," replied Scott defensively.

"I'm asking 'cause that girl is like my own flesh and blood. I promised her daddy I'd look after her and that's what I'm going to do," emphasized the older man. "I know you didn't plan on coming here, and I get the feeling that part of what you're saying is true. But you and that partner of yours ain't no prospectors, and I want to know what your intentions are," stated Schuster, and now the rifle was pointed dead center.

If it hadn't been for the serious look on the older man's face and the gun in his hands, Scott would have laughed at the man's old-fashioned protectiveness. But Scott knew it sprang from a deep love for the girl and a desire to protect her. Maybe that's why he just couldn't keep it up.

"You have to know I mean Lisa no harm," said Scott as he moved over toward his saddle, with the rifle in Schuster's hands tracking him all the way.

"That may be," said Schuster, "but she's setting her hat for you and that's trouble. Besides, you're not fooling me, you are all turned inside out yourself."

Scott slowly pulled out his boot knife and turned his saddle over and began to cut the heavy stitching under the pommel. He reached in and pulled out the five-pointed silver star and the heavy paper commission book stating his authority as an Operative of the Secret Service and bearing the gold seal of the President of the United States and signed by the Secretary of the Treasury.

"This will tell you who I am and what I do," said Scott, turning to face Schuster.

Schuster laid the gun down and took the silver badge and commission book from Scott.   "The President says you are worthy of trust and confidence. (*See Footnotes 3 and 4.*) I guess you can't get a better recommendation than that," he replied.[3]

"I've read about government lawmen like you in the papers that Lisa gets from back East but never expected to see one out here," said Schuster.   "I did hear about some lawmen up in Wyoming that busted up a big land swindle, but I thought it was probably U.S. Marshals."[4]

"It was Secret Service operatives, but not Miguel and me," said Scott.

"I guess you were right not to let us know exactly who you are or what you're up to, but she's not gonna be happy to see you leave, and you are leaving, aren't you?" asked Schuster.

"I really don't want to leave, but I've got a job to do," said Scott. "I never expected this to happen. I'd like to stay awhile and do some serious courting, but that's not possible. Lisa is special, and you are right about the feelings. I've never even thought about this kind of closeness with any other woman. I don't even know how to describe it," Scott confessed.

"I'd like to tell you I'm sorry I doubted you, but we both know better," shrugged Schuster.

They shook hands and just like that, they both knew the matter was settled.

---

[3] See Photos #3 and #4
[4] The phrase "Worthy of Trust and Confidence" still appears on the current Special Agent Commission Book.

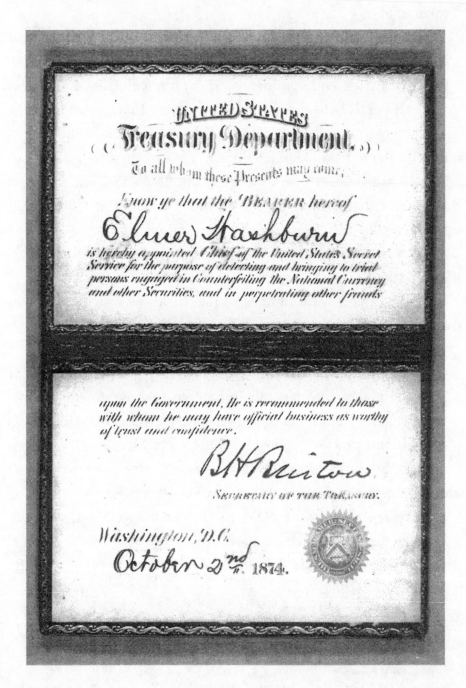

Commission Book

Silver Badge

CHAPTER 25

Scott slowly recounted the story of his counterfeiting case, the shooting in Leadville, the things they learned in Glenrock about the Two Aces Cattle and Mine Company, and the ambush that wounded Miguel.

"I heard of this Two Aces outfit; they bought an old mine over east a-ways. It was a claim Lisa's dad found a few years ago," exclaimed Schuster. "I heard they were bringing in some new type of mining equipment that would make old mines like that one profitable. It was originally a small operation backed by a syndicate from New York. They made a nice profit, but it wasn't some kind of mother lode. When the easy gold was mined out, they moved on. The place is a little off the beaten path," stated Schuster.

"How long will it take me to get over there?" asked Scott.

"If you go the way you and Miguel were going, probably a day and a half or two full days with wagons, but there's a lot quicker way," replied Schuster.

"How's that?" asked Scott.

"There's several old trails you can take that could get you there in a day at the longest, assuming you don't get lost. We've got maps in the house that the old man made, but I'll be glad to ride with you and lend a hand. You are going to definitely need a guide."

"I sure could use a hand," said Scott, "but it's just too dangerous. If something happened to you, Lisa would never forgive me."

"So if I let you go off alone, now that I know what you are doing and something happened to you, you think she would ever forgive me?" asked Schuster incredulously. "I take it you're not planning on telling her what you're up to?"

"No, I can't tell her because I think she'd be hell-bent to come," said Scott.

"You're cutting a mighty-big chunk for one man to chew," said Schuster, "especially since you know there's two of them on the prowl and at least one other you don't even know."

"All I'm going to do is locate where these fellas are doing their printing, and then I can get the Army to help me arrest them," said Scott. "It really shouldn't be all that dangerous. Once we get them arrested, they'll tell us all we need to know to round up the others. The threat of a long sentence in a Federal prison tends to make people talkative."

Schuster laughed. "Right, it won't be dangerous . . . that's why your partner is lying in there all shot up!"

Scott didn't know what to say, so he just shrugged his shoulders. It wasn't really the way he liked to work cases, but this time he didn't have many options.

"Well, at least let me guide you part of the way. I'll not have you getting yourself killed falling off some trail ledge. The maps are amazingly accurate but the weather does make some changes over time," stated Schuster. "We can tell Lisa and the family I'm going over to help you with your claim and come right back."

"Will it fool them?" asked Scott.

"Sure enough," shrugged Frank. "Carl and Albert are good men but they are civilized ranchers and breeders. They know a lot of book learning, a lot about animals, especially cattle, but not so much about people. Albert actually went to school back East. I'm the only one that even looked sideways at your yarn about being a prospector."

"Lisa maybe . . ."

Both men looked up startled as Lisa swung open the barn door and stepped inside.

"Well, what are you two up to, gossiping over the back fence?" asked Lisa, giving both men a questioning look.

"Frank, here was offering to show me an easy way to reach our claim," replied Will, immediately regretting his reply as a disappointed look crossed her face. "But if you don't object, I'd like to come back and give you a hand with your horses in order to repay your kindness in taking care of Miguel."

"The only objection I have is to Uncle Frank's big mouth in offering to help you leave," said Lisa bluntly. She stomped to the tack room at the end of the barn to get her saddle. Uncle Frank took the opportunity to make good his getaway, leaving Will to brave her anger. But when she returned with her saddle, she was nice as could be, a fact that left Will Scott totally confused.

They rode all afternoon, just as before, with the exception that Scott was again riding Miguel's horse Torreon instead of his own. When they stopped at the spring to water the horses, she came into his arms and gave him such a kiss that it left them both breathless.

"That's so you'll know you're supposed to come back," she breathed, stepping away and swinging up on her horse.

All Scott was capable of doing was standing speechless as she cantered down the trail back toward the ranch house.

CHAPTER 26

When he got back to the ranch, Uncle Frank was waiting for him. Schuster took Will into the library and showed him a very large bookcase containing bound journals.

"Good Lord," said Will. "How many are there?"

"I never really counted them, but I think there are over two-hundred", replied Frank. "The old man used Army ordnance maps as a beginning, but then the routes he took are very detailed and most times you only see some general landmarks in common with the Army maps. He always sort of indexed his trails and travels with a starting and ending point on the Army maps, though. That way when his details ended, you could tell where you were by the Army map. I pulled out the journal for this area. Actually, its two journals, not because of the distance, but because of all of the geological information he recorded in this area."

Will nodded. "I know there has been a great deal of mining in this part of the state, but I thought it was just some old prospector stumbling on an area and then the boom that followed news of the strike."

Frank laughed. "Oh sure, there was some of that, but very few people made it big that way. Even most of those who did managed to lose it all eventually. Syndicates backed by people like Rockefeller and J. P. Morgan were the ones who really profited. They would hire trained geologists to scour the boom areas and locate and buy prime places for real mines. Then with their money, they would sink mines deep, use big equipment and build crushers to extract every ounce from the ore. Usually, all the gold fever fools who rushed out to the so-called gold fields, ended up working in the mines and living in company houses."

"That's not a very pretty picture," said Scott.

"No, it's not," agreed Schuster. "Plus, those big mines really make a mess of some real pretty country. Lisa's dad was very good with money, and he found this valley and surrounding area early on and was determined to own it. He'd use some of what the syndicates paid him to buy acres, and then he would get them to buy big chunks of this valley and give it to him in payment for his services. Some of it was government land, but the powerful syndicates had no trouble getting title to it with all their lawyers and friendly politicians. Carl, Sr. pinpointed so many good mining sites that he was in constant demand. We crisscrossed all over this state, and he recorded all the promising spots we surveyed. A bunch of times he would already be familiar with an area one of the syndicates was interested in. After the initial strike, he would wait a while and then come in here and look up coordinates and wire them back East."

"Did you do all this with him?" asked Will.

"Not just him. Lisa's mother came with us before the kids came, and then a lot of times, she would bring the kids along. She was an amazing woman, raised in the city and on a big farm back East, but her family was blue blood all the way. She was a mix of city and country girl. Yeah, we made quite a trio for more than 25 years," said Frank. "We really are a family, and that's why I'm so protective. Besides, we all own this ranch together; it's called a corporation. It was something some of those big business men back East convinced the old man to do. There's a lawyer in Denver that Lisa or Albert sends reports to once a year and he handles all the legal stuff. All we have to do is ranch, and it's been working for a long time."

"That is really quite amazing, especially out West here," marveled Will.

"I'll get all the pack stuff together we need for the trip. I'm sure you have your own personal stuff together," said Frank.

"As if you didn't know!" laughed Will.

Supper that evening was something to remember. Lisa wore a cream dress that offset her dark hair, and everyone at the supper table could see that she and Will only had eyes for each other. After supper, they all went upstairs and ate apple pie with an improving Miguel who himself actually ate a whole piece of pie. Louisa pronounced her patient on the road to recovery and shooed them all out of the room so Miguel could go to sleep. Everyone went to their rooms and Will Scott fell asleep thinking of Lisa and didn't wake up until Frank Schuster rousted him out of bed at dawn.

After seeing Will and Uncle Frank ride off, Lisa came into the kitchen and collapsed into a chair. "What am I going to do, Louisa? The man is like a magnet to me; I can't wait to see him, talk to him, and Lord knows, kiss him."

Louisa came over to the table slowly and sat down. "The heart is a funny thing; it leads you sometimes where you never expected to go, niña," she murmured.

"Did Miguel say anything at all?" asked Lisa.

"No, he is very slippery, and when I think I might be getting close to something, he says he is tired and pretends to sleep."

"Maybe we shouldn't feed him for a day and maybe that would loosen his tongue," laughed Louisa.

"They definitely have secrets that neither is willing to share. I showed him the turquoise diggings," said Lisa.

"Madre de Dios," exclaimed Louisa, crossing herself, knowing how the family felt about the place.

"Funny thing was, he said he had never seen turquoise in rock like that. Any miner with any experience at all would have seen some turquoise in its natural form. I am not willing to spend the rest of my life with a man that is not truly honest, no matter what the attraction. I'm not settling for less than what mom and dad had," fumed Lisa. "Thanks for talking, mamacita. If he doesn't do right, I'm at peace with letting him ride away, but I'll be darn if I let him get off easy."

"I will say a prayer that he does right," answered Louisa.

"Well, now that that's settled, I'm going out and be with my horses. Nothing will change until they get back," said Lisa.

CHAPTER 27

They rode for half-a-day over trails that hadn't been used in a long time. Occasionally, Schuster would refer to the maps for reference points and landmarks.

"This here is where you're headed," said Frank, spreading the map out on a rock while they both munched on the grub Lisa insisted that they take. "This claim sits at the north end of a small canyon. There's a fair sized stream running down the middle of the place. The old mine sits off to the side some."

Scott looked at the map and laughed. "I've read a few maps, and I don't know any map signs that indicate what you just told me."

"The maps are good, but the real facts like I told you are in these," said Schuster, walking to his horse and pulling a leather bound journal from his saddlebag. "These journals tell details like that about nearly every place the old man surveyed. I looked the place up last night just to refresh my memory."

"It's no wonder he did so well in the mining business. I never heard of anybody doing this kind of planning. I always thought half of mining was luck," laughed Scott.

"The old man always said it was luck, but with the right surveying, it was the same luck you'd have playing poker with a deck half full of aces," laughed Schuster.

They mounted up and moved on, single file most of the time due to the narrowness of the trail. It was some wild but beautiful country that had never been ruined by the mining so common in other parts of the state. Scott saw the bouncing tails of mule deer through the trees and marveled as always at their size and speed. "This countryside is really something," said Scott, moving alongside Schuster as the trail widened out.

"There's never been any mining in this area?" asked Scott.

"Nope, it's too rugged for one thing to interest anybody but a single prospector. The old man always said the Lord gave this area all the natural beauty and put all the gold someplace else. Even if he believed or even knew there was gold here, I'm not sure he would have ever told anybody," mused Schuster. "Besides that, we own most of the land we've been riding on."

"Good Lord," exclaimed Scott, "how many acres is the place?"

Schuster grinned, "I don't know. It's actually better to tell you in miles, but even I'm not totally sure."

It was late in the afternoon when they finally stopped to make camp.

"We're only about two to three miles from that claim," said Schuster. "I figured we might as well see it in daylight tomorrow morning."

"You're right about that," said Scott. "I've got a lot of questions about these hombres. It's one thing to go to all the trouble of making counterfeit money, but you've got to be able to use it. Only five of these bills have shown up so far. That's not what this operation was set up to do. These fellas must have some big plans," reflected Scott. "We were following wagons with a lot of printing supplies. In fact, that amount of supplies would support the largest counterfeit operation I've ever seen. I would guess that they had made a preliminary printing in order to perfect their plates and calibrate their equipment. Unfortunately, that's sort of the same process the government uses."

"Beats me," said Schuster. "There's not that much money spent around here. Most of the money is in the U.S. Assay Office in Leadville."

"What do they do with the gold dust and bars from the mines?" asked Scott.

"They store the gold for a while and then they eventually ship it back East. The Army usually comes out and takes care of that," said Schuster.

"Do they pay cash for the gold when they get it from the miners?" asked Scott.

"Well, they used to in the old days, but I heard that now they give fellas some piece of paper and then they go to the bank for their money," said Schuster. "There's not that many small guys anymore. Like I told you, most mining is done by big syndicates who bring their gold in by the wagon full once a month maybe. Then they credit their account at the bank so the mine owners can pay their expenses."

"That bank must have a lot of money in it," mused Scott.

"I reckon," nodded Schuster.

They built a small campfire with dry wood underneath a rock overhang that would break up any smoke the fire would make. Scott didn't think these crooks would have any reason to be especially expecting company, but his lack of carefulness, at least in his mind, had almost gotten Miguel killed. Schuster fussed around the campfire making coffee and fixing supper, while in the growing dusk, Will Scott read the old man's journal about the specific area where they were going. The script was broad and flowing and Scott could almost feel what the old man must have felt when he was describing the land. The descriptions were as detailed and as precise as you would expect from an engineer—full of small things like descriptions of the flowers or the way the sunset looked against the sky that clearly showed the writer's love of what he was seeing.

"Pretty strong stuff, huh?" drawled Schuster.

Scott started at the sound of Frank's voice, having been lost in the written words.

"Some powerful writing," said Scott. "None of that drugstore novel stuff. His writing is so descriptive. This is how the West really is."

"Or was," mused Schuster.

"If people back East ever read this kind of stuff, they'd all want to head West," laughed Scott.

"There are so many folks out here now. I thought they already did!" growled Schuster.

They pitched in to clean up after supper, and after banking their fire, they both settled into their bedrolls full and content.

CHAPTER 28

Two thousand miles or so away, the spring night was cool, but nothing like as crisp as the night Will Scott and Frank Schuster would be experiencing. Instead of going to sleep, people were moving about Washington, D.C., their days extending into the night. The two government officials could see carriages moving in the streets below them, but they were too deep in conversation to really notice. The two men had known each other in college, and since arriving in D.C. had engineered a number of land swindles out West. Maddox had brought the other man in on the counterfeit plan so there was nothing to tie Maddox to anything west of the Potomac. Stang sent all the messages out West.

"It's not my fault the money showed up," insisted the short red-faced man, who by day demanded that his employees address him as Mr. Secretary. Behind his back, the same group of employees called him "Dumpling". Wilbur Stang, Secretary of the Interior, was not popular with his employees, to say the least. He was pompous and overbearing with everyone, but he was especially disliked by the ladies who often found him a little quick with his hands.

"It was your responsibility," boomed Treasury Secretary Maddox, turning from the window.

"Fredericks and Simpkins took care of the man who stole the counterfeit and spent it in Leadville," insisted Stang.

"But what about the agents who were on their trail?" asked

Maddox.

"They swear they killed the Mexican," weaseled Stang.

"They also insisted he was alone! They should have waited until they had them both," insisted Maddox.

"This fella Scott doesn't know too much. Maybe killing the Mexican will have scared him off," pondered Stang. "Besides, they know what Scott looks like and they'll be ready for him."

"Don't be stupid. If anything, he'll be even more determined. Scott is one of the best Secret Service operatives, and the investigation is centered around Glenrock and Silver Creek," stated Maddox.

"You always said you could handle that part of it," mocked Stang. "You said how easy it would be with Taylor as Chief of the Secret Service."

"Yes, I'll admit that Taylor was not what I expected. Those stupid stories and that get-up . . . I thought they were parlor tricks. Who would've thought he was genuine," mused Maddox. "I should have never appointed him, but his predecessor was too suspicious of everyone. Besides, I appointed him years ago, way before we got this opportunity."

"What's he going to do next?" asked Stang.

"He says he is going to solve this even if he has to send out every operative in the Secret Service," replied Maddox.

"Maybe we should change our plans," stated Stang.

"No," said Maddox, setting his whiskey glass down with a bang. "Everything is going too good. The money is extremely good. Scott is good, but he is really at a disadvantage now, alone and outgunned. Taylor is a problem, but I can keep a watch on him and learn what's going on. I am his boss after all," reflected Maddox with a smug grin. "I just found out that the

BEP Chief invited him on the trip to Silver Creek. I'll know if he hears from Scott."

"Has Taylor said anything about the two missing brothers?" asked Stang.

"No, the Bureau of Engraving and Printing was hot to trot when they discovered the brothers were gone, but they suspected an inside tip-off. They were too embarrassed to tell the Secret Service and initiate a big manhunt with wanted posters," laughed Maddox. "I doubt anyone outside the Bureau of Engraving and Printing has ever heard of those two brothers. I want you to send this message to Andrew in Glenrock," said Maddox, handing Stang several notes. "I want him to know Taylor is coming out with us and to keep his eyes peeled for Scott."

As soon as the little man left, Maddox began to reflect on the overall situation. It was a good plan, he thought to himself, and it was going along relatively smoothly. The stupid thief and his friend who passed the counterfeit were dead and buried along with the Mexican. Scott was definitely slowed, if not finished. The last report indicated they were getting close to finishing the printing, and his cousin Andrew was running everything out West. Andrew was his first cousin and they had been like brothers since they were kids. They were the same but opposite. When they were in school, anytime Maddox had a problem with another boy, he would bide his time until he could sneak up behind and smash the kid when nobody was looking. Andrew, on the other hand, would let his temper get the best of him and hit another kid in the mouth in front of God and everybody. His uncle's money had kept Andrew out of official trouble. Money went to victims, principals and teachers to smooth everything over. Not to mention, everyone was scared of the crazy kid.

When Maddox went off to college, Andrew went with him — not to go to school, just to be with his cousin. Maddox was his only friend, and by then the uncle had disowned his brawling, drinking, womanizing offspring. Unfortunately, for both of them, their respective fathers had wasted most of the family fortune. While in school, Maddox had a small stipend from his grandmother, but he was extremely envious of his fellow students, most of whom had plenty of money. Andrew wanted to just stick a gun in their smug faces and take their money, but Maddox showed him how it was much easier to cheat and swindle students and the townspeople as well. They ran crooked card games, tricked the unsuspecting into bogus land/gold mine deals out West, and even resorted to a little blackmail. Andrew was always the one out front, while Maddox stayed in the background orchestrating everything. For most, it would not have worked, but for them, it was perfect. Andrew liked the action, the occasional violence and the risk, while Maddox loved the plotting and scheming behind their actions. Very, very few people knew the two were acquainted, much less related. Andrew gradually evolved into a slick, polished criminal who only resorted to violence as a last resort, and then he usually had someone else do it. Back then, it had been the Italian kid. Now he had Fredericks and Simpkins. The Italian kid did whatever Andrew told him. Fredericks and Simpkins also followed orders, but were just plain mean.

Maddox studied banking and finance at Princeton and pored over every news story about the giants of business, such as the Vanderbilts, Rockefellers and J. P. Morgan. He felt himself a "robber baron" at heart, willing to do whatever it took to make money.

CHAPTER 29

John Bell had been watching the Secretary of the Interior on and off, since it seemed to be a waste of time. He was shocked when the Secretary stayed late one night, and when he left the building, he didn't take one of the carriages that was parked at the corner. Finally, Bell thought to himself.

Stang walked several blocks away from his office and then hailed an empty carriage. Bell had to hustle to get his own carriage and told the driver to follow. When Stang's carriage made the final turn toward The Treasury building, Bell stopped his carriage and hopped out, giving the man a $5.00 coin. "Thanks, mate," said the cabbie, but Bell was already gone.

Bell saw Stang go in the building, but didn't intend to follow. There wouldn't be many employees left, but even so, there was always a chance someone would know him. Besides, he had no doubt where "Dumpling" was headed. Bell could see lights burning in Secretary Maddox's office, so he found a dark doorway where he could see the corner office and the front door of the building. No more than an hour later, Bell saw Stang exit the Treasury Building, walking briskly. Two blocks over, he again hailed a passing taxi carriage. Expecting the move, John Bell was already standing next to a parked taxi carriage. Showing his badge and promising a big tip, Bell ordered the cabbie to follow Stang.

The two cabs traveled a good twenty blocks or so to an area with pubs and cafes. It was not a bad area, just not the kind of neighborhood frequented by politicians. Stang stopped in the middle of the block in front of a Western Union storefront and obviously had told the cabbie to wait. Bell got out at the end of the block, tipped the carriage driver generously, and sent him on his way. Bell hustled down the opposite of the street just in time to see Stang hand the telegraph operator a bottle of whiskey. The two men obviously knew each other. Bell saw Stang give the man an envelope and some money. After shaking hands, Stang came out and got back in his carriage and headed off.

Bell decided to take a chance and check out the telegraph operator. As he approached the office, Bell was debating identifying himself and asking to see the message. The bottle of whiskey disturbed him, and as he got close, he could see the operator going to the telegraph key. Bell knew the operators were supposed to log in their sent telegrams and account for the fees. When Bell saw the telegrapher ignoring his log book and start sending a message, he just kept walking.

The next morning when he got to the office, John Bell gave Eddie a high sign and they both made their way separately to the Chief's office.

"Top of the morning, Doris," said Eddie. Doris just raised an eyebrow and pointed to the Chief's open door.

John Bell was already there, so Eddie shut the door.

"I finally got something," said John. He related the previous night's events to the Chief and Eddie.

"Well, they're sticking true to form," said the Chief.

"I wish I could have gotten a copy of that telegram," said Bell. "I could see that the operator didn't log it in, so there's no use going back today."

"Chief," Eddie said. "I really think you should let us go out West. We could go separate."

"I'm not taking a chance," said the Chief. "I still think we will hear from Will before I have to leave."

"I had an idea," said Eddie. "If the brothers left town with White, they had to get their printing supplies somewhere. I'll go to some of the printing supply houses around here and see if they have shipped anything interesting. Also, I'll telegraph the Chicago office and see if they can check out things there. If we're lucky, maybe they bought stuff on their way West."

"Get the Denver office on it, too," said the Chief. "They only know Will is on a special assignment for the Chief's office."

"We'll let you know when we hear back," said Eddie, as he and Bell left the Chief's office.

CHAPTER 30

Scott and Schuster both woke with the first light, eager to get underway. Within two hours of dawn, they had positioned themselves among a jumble of boulders overlooking the claim. With the field glasses, Scott could see the stream and what looked like the entrance to a mine in good detail. The mine didn't look like any new activity was going on, but there was a brand new building as big as a good-sized barn sitting next to the stream. Attached to it was a small shed, and Will could see a small steam engine and a flywheel and belt that ran from a shed through the wall of the building.

"That's definitely not mining equipment," mused Schuster.

"No, the steam engine is used to power the machinery inside. They probably have a couple of large presses and a paper cutter in there. The belt from the steam engine goes through a series of gears and flywheels to power the machinery," answered Scott.

"Somebody is spending a lot of money to do this counterfeiting," reflected Schuster.

"Yeah, most counterfeiting operations are not like this. Usually it's one or two printers that make up a run of their own brand of money. Their big problem is how to circulate it," informed Scott.

"Where do they get the plates?" asked Frank.

"They generally make the plates themselves if they are serious. Sometimes they get an engraver and pay him to do the work, but that's small time, not much volume. It all begins with the engraving. It's done by hand using dragon's blood to etch the design into a metal plate. Cut too deep and there's too much ink on the paper—too shallow, not enough. The counterfeit I saw was almost perfect. Somebody down there is a master engraver. An operation this size will need a large number of plates," stated Scott. "They are usually copper, and the pressure of the printing press wears them out pretty quick. They usually engrave sections and make multiple runs through the press. You have to be very meticulous or there is a lot of waste."

At that moment, they heard the small steam engine fire up. Over the next several hours, they observed the comings and goings of the counterfeiters. Scott made notes in a journal of his own describing the buildings and each man working at the claim. It was easy but boring work. Scott's hands shook as he noted the descriptions of his two old friends, Fredericks and Simpkins. Knowing they tried to kill Miguel made Scott want to use his rifle and kill them where they stood, but he resisted the temptation. The two wagons and their drivers appeared to have dropped off their freight and gone back to Glenrock.

"I figure we'll be riding to get the Army pretty soon?" asked Schuster.

"I wish it were that easy. Have you seen any counterfeit money?" asked Scott.

"No, but that's not mining equipment down there, and those are the two fellas that ambushed Miguel," fumed Schuster.

"That means we know they're liars and attempted murderers, but that's about all we know for sure," replied Scott. "I have to make a statement to a Federal Judge and swear that I know certain things for sure before the cavalry will come charging up on somebody's private property," continued Scott. "I have to be with them when they raid a place. The Army really doesn't have the authority to arrest people for counterfeiting."

"We just gonna ride down there and ask them fellas to show us?" asked Schuster sarcastically.

Scott laughed and replied, "No, we're gonna see what they're doing, figure out their pattern, and then I'm gonna go down and sneak a look."

"Well, now, I like that idea," said Schuster, shaking his head. "Lisa will kill me if something happens to you."

With his field glasses, Scott could see two people moving inside the building besides his two old enemies.

"I make five hombres," said Frank, slipping down beside Scott.

"Yeah, me, too," said Scott. "I didn't get a real good look at the two others, though, and they haven't come outside again."

"Well, it's past noon; they all ought to come out soon for grub," pondered Schuster.

"I can see that the guy in the red shirt runs the camp. He's been stirring something in that pot on the fire and I swear I can smell it," said Scott, chewing on some hardtack from his saddlebags.

"Here's some jerky. I'll swap you for the hardtack," said Frank, handing Scott some of the dried beef.

As if on cue, the door of the building opened and out trooped the four men. Scott began to note the descriptions of the two unknown men in his journal. The one was of medium build with dark hair and appeared to Scott to be about thirty-five years old. He was somewhat stooped and appeared to wear spectacles. The man was wearing a printer's apron and his shirt sleeves were held up with black garters.

The other man was older and what hair he had was gray. He was short and heavy and even from a distance, Scott could see the man wore heavy glasses. The man was extremely pale, and his clothes appeared to be neat and clean. Scott noticed that the man wiped his plate and utensils clean before accepting a ladle of stew from the cook.

Even from this distance, Scott could tell these two men weren't Westerners.

"Do you recognize these fellas?" asked Schuster.

"No, I don't know either one, but if I can get to a telegraph, maybe someone in Washington can help us with that," replied Scott, busily writing down a detailed description of the two men.

"You gonna go down there after nightfall?" wondered Schuster.

"Maybe. We're gonna see if they post any guards or if anybody's sleeping where they're working," replied Scott.

"How late do you think they'll work?" asked Schuster.

"Not that late, although a lot of printers work at night because it's cooler," replied Scott. "But out here, they only have lantern light, so it may be hard to see, and both seem to be wearing heavy spectacles."

The counterfeiters ate their lunch and wasted no time going back inside the building and leaving the cook to clean up. The older camp boss seemed to sweat a lot, as Scott could see the man frequently wiping his brow with what appeared to be a white silk handkerchief. The afternoon dragged on for Scott and Schuster. The counterfeiters appeared outside only a few times and then only for a drink of water or to visit the privy. Scott made notes of the activity but knew what really mattered was what he could see when he got inside the building. Fredericks and Simpkins didn't spend a lot of time inside the building.   They tended to other things around the camp, occasionally sitting down with the cook and drinking coffee. It was late afternoon when the man wearing the printer's apron came to the door and called out for Fredericks and Simpkins. He had a piece of paper in his hands, but before Scott could get the glasses up, he was back inside.   Scott swore under his breath, rousing a slumbering Schuster.

"What happened?" asked Frank.

"Nothing really, but the young one was at the door with a sheet, but I couldn't get a look," replied Scott.

"You woke me up for that?" asked Schuster.

"You woke yourself up with all that snoring," laughed Scott. "Why don't you go back to our camp and rustle us up some grub? I'm gonna watch what they do at dark and then I'll be there."

"Be careful," grumbled Schuster, as he headed back to their primitive camp.

Scott's prediction came partly true. The counterfeiters came out before dusk and again ate their meal in full view. But after supper, Fredericks and the older man walked over to the other small building that Scott assumed was the bunk house and went inside. The younger, spectacled man took the coffee pot and a cup from the cook and went back inside the main building. Scott saw the inside of the building lighting up as the man walked around igniting a number of kerosene lanterns. Scott withdrew and headed back to their camp.

CHAPTER 31

"I**t's** about time you showed up," grumbled Schuster, as Scott came into the camp. "The coffee is hot and here's a plate of rabbit stew."

"What did the rabbit do, wander into camp and you snored him to death?" replied Scott, doubling over with laughter.

"Very funny," said the older man, keeping his head down so Scott couldn't see the grin. "Don't eat it if you don't want it."

"It's too good not to eat," said Scott, savoring a mouthful of the stew. "How did you get the rabbit?"

"I set a snare down by the stream and got one late this morning and another this afternoon," said Schuster.

"I was just beginning to get used to that hardtack and jerky. Now my stomach knows better again," laughed Scott. "It's good you cooked this because it's gonna be a long night. The younger man, I'm sure he's the printer, seems to be working tonight. It's surprising, but a big advantage for us. The older one is most likely the engraver. I'm gonna sneak down there and see what I can see while you keep me covered."

"Suppose something goes wrong and they spot you?" asked Schuster.

"Well, then you start shooting and carrying on. Maybe we can fool 'em into thinking we're the fifth cavalry, and they'll surrender before we tell them any different," said Scott.

"You call that a plan, you being a military man and all?" wondered a worried Schuster. "It's a very long shot, even with a good rifle, and what we have is not made for long range."

"I never claimed it was a perfect plan, but if I can just see the money inside, we can bring the Army in," replied Scott. "They've got to move it sooner or later. That money is not worth anything just sitting there."

They ate their supper pretty much in silence. There wasn't a whole lot to say about what they were going to do. After eating, Scott checked his pistol and rifle while Schuster did the same. They hiked to their earlier vantage point pretty much in silence. Using the field glasses, they went over Scott's route through the rocks and down to the outlaw camp until each was sure what the other one was to do.

"I'll stash my rifle part way down. I'll need both hands climbing around in the dark," said Will.

"You be careful," cautioned Schuster.

"Careful is my middle name, didn't I tell you?" said Scott, giving the older man's hand a firm handshake.

"If there's no trouble, I'll meet you back at camp at dawn," replied Schuster.

Scott returned a half-salute and slipped away into the darkness.

Schuster moved a quarter mile to the highest point overlooking the camp and tried to get comfortable on the boulders.

After leaving their spot, Scott worked his way east until he crossed a wash that led to the rough game trail he planned to follow. Despite the darkness, the trail was not too difficult and was almost as the old man had described it in his journal. Scott didn't think this path was known to those in the camp. He'd had trouble locating it by sight, and if it hadn't been the old man's way into the area, it would probably still be unknown. The stars were up but not the moon, and Scott moved from landmark to landmark until he was in the small valley east of his original vantage point. He eased onto the top of a large boulder, lying flat, and surveyed the camp in front of him. The sleeping quarters were dark, and try as he might, Scott could see no one moving around the camp. The other building was a different story. There was light coming from every window. In the quiet, over the noise of the small steam engine, Scott could hear the unmistakable thump of a platen press striking its images onto paper. This is too easy, thought Scott as he shifted his weight to move from his perch atop the boulder. He sensed, rather than really felt, the weight across his calf just above his boot. He slowly turned his head and watched a four-foot rattler glide over his calf and down the boulder on his search for a nightly meal. Scott's whole body shook as he wiped cold sweat from his forehead and tried to calm his shocked nerves. Once he could, Scott slipped off the boulder in the opposite direction of the snake and began working his way toward the workshop. As he moved closer, Scott could clearly see there was another man inside the building next to the one where they were printing. He immediately recognized him as the cook, and Scott could see him feeding the steam engine burner. Scott could clearly see the top of the press as the round plate rotated, picking up the ink onto the plate with one stroke and then pressing the inked image onto the paper with the other. He hunkered down behind a small boulder and pondered an opportunity to move the final distance. Occasionally, the platen press would stop and Scott could see the printer moving around the machine servicing it and making adjustments. He once saw the printer with a printing frame and knew he was changing the plate.   Scott could occasionally hear snatches of their conversation, but not enough to really understand anything. He was certain they were printing money; there was no other conclusion, but he had to be certain.   His honesty and pride would have it no other way.

The cook moved out of his sight, and Scott heard the man open the door and then saw him shuffle around the building and feed several pieces of wood into the steam engine burner. When the man moved back inside and the press started again, Scott knew it would be his chance.   At the first stroke of the press, Scott was up and moving toward the window. He stayed just outside the square of light that shone through the window, but he could see clearly the activity going on inside. He quickly took in the sight of a large press rotating around and striking an image onto the waiting paper.   He saw the shiny copper plates engraved in $100 denominations.   He saw another small press with numbering wheels which would be used to print the serial numbers.   There were an extremely large number of stacks of paper, most of which were at least partially printed.   The opposite corner of the room, which he could only partially see, must have been where the engraver was working.   There were large sketches of the Monroe $100 bills tacked on the wall, as well as other sketches depicting various portions of the bill.   It only took a few moments for these sights to sink in and for Scott to turn and sneak away.   The return trip to the game trail leading to the top of the canyon was without incident.   Just as he started up the path, Will realized that it was slowly growing light.   He had been so intent with his mission that he had almost lost track of time.   He really picked up his pace.   There was no way he wanted to spend an entire day hiding behind a boulder to avoid detection.

Will made it up the trail with time to spare. Back at their camp, he started a small fire, and by the time Schuster arrived at daybreak, the coffee was hot and Will was busy writing the details of what he had seen in his own journal.

"How long you been here?" groused the older man.

"Not long, why?" asked Scott.

"I swear I could never see you even though I had a perfect view of the camp," replied Schuster. "Besides, I'd be madder than a wet hen thinking you'd been here taking it easy while I was camped out on a cold rock!" he said, breaking into a big grim. "I hope it was worth it."

"It was," grinned Scott. "They are doing it all right there. I could see plates and lots of paper. There appeared to be a large amount of currency finished and cut. This whole thing is very unusual. The place is set up like a commercial print shop with belt driven equipment. Normally, all the equipment is manually operated. From what I could see, the amount of counterfeit is staggering."

Schuster slapped his knee and exclaimed, "Well, let's go get the cavalry!"

"Hold on there, Chief Sitting Bull, it's not that easy," laughed Scott. "First, we ride to the nearest telegraph line to send a message to my Chief, and then he will go through proper channels and a message will be sent to Fort Gordon for a detachment."

Schuster's mouth dropped. "That will take a couple of days, at least. Why don't we just sneak down there and get the drop on these hombres?"

"'Cause there's no guarantee we can do that. And even if we did, we can't just ride off and leave all that money there!" replied Scott.

"I never knew being a law man could be so complicated," frowned Schuster.

"It's not usually, but everything about this case is different—the quality of the counterfeit, where they're printing it, and what they obviously know about us trying to catch them. Yes, sir, real different. Let's catch a quick nap and then head for that telegraph wire," replied Scott.

CHAPTER 32

They both slept soundly for several hours before the bright sun woke them. Using the old man's map and journal, they figured the easiest route to the telegraph wire and then mounted up. With any luck, they figured to be at the telegraph by nightfall. The ride was an easy one for both the men and the horses. There was not much steep climbing, and they rested the horses several times. Scott spent much of the ride thinking about Lisa and what the future might bring. It was an uncomfortable feeling for him. He usually didn't plan real far ahead, but he found himself thinking about how much he missed her and couldn't wait to see her. The problem was, he loved the life he was living; at least he had before he met her. Now, he wasn't real sure.

"I'm glad your horse is paying attention to where he's going. Your mind is obviously someplace else. You haven't said a word in the last hour," grumbled Schuster.

Scott reddened at the older man's criticism. "I'm making serious plans to capture these counterfeiters," he said.

"That's the way women are, son; they get inside you and drive you crazy. They don't really mean to, but they do, especially the really special ones like Lisa," said Schuster.

"You ever been married, Frank?" asked Scott.

"Yeah, my wife died of consumption many years back. I got a real decent widow-lady I see over in Leadville now and then, though," answered Frank.

"I never really found one that I wanted to stay with very long. What with the Army and this job, I never really thought about settling down," reflected Scott.

"Well, things change as you get older. I still want to see what's over the next ridge, but just not quite bad enough to get up and do it," laughed Frank. "Besides, I kind of like the ranch and being part of a family."

"That Lisa really did something to me. I can't wait three days to get back and just be there. It's not something I'm used to. I just hope she'll let me stay awhile when we're done with this," moaned Scott.

Schuster grinned widely. "I reckon she'll let you stay a little while. But I can tell you that we are both going to have a real problem when we get back."

"What do you mean?" asked Will.

"That girl is really smart, and we kind of steamrolled right over her and got out of there. Once she has a chance to think about things a little, she is going to know we are a couple of big liars," said Schuster.

"I guess we are going to have to tell her the truth and hope she understands," replied Scott.

"I just hope she's madder at you than she is at me," growled Schuster.

They got to the telegraph wire in late afternoon, using Will's Army map to make sure the wire was truly active. Schuster started a small fire while Will tapped into the wire. After hooking into the wire, Will sat down and wrote out the coded message he wanted to send.

"Isn't it kind of risky sending this message to Washington when you know there's a fox in that henhouse?" asked Frank.

"Not even a sly old fox will be able to figure this message out," replied Scott. "You see, I have this wheel," said Scott, holding up two heavy pieces of paper in the shape of a wheel. On the outside of the wheel were all the letters of the alphabet and numbers one through ten. On the smaller wheel were all the letters of the alphabet and the numbers one through ten.

"What in tarnation is that?" asked Frank.

"It's a wheel code system. You see, you take this big wheel and then you take this smaller wheel, which again has all the letters and numbers on it with an open space. See how the numbers and letters are all mixed around on each wheel? Then you tell the person you're sending a message to that you are using, for example, A on the wheel. Align the open space to A, and then reading off the inner wheel, you code your message. See, in code, the letter A is really O and the number 5 is F," explained Scott.

"So what's to keep somebody else from having one of these wheels?" asked Frank.

"Because there's only one other that matches this one," replied Scott. "The letters and numbers were just picked any which way by the Chief. Each Secret Service operative has a wheel, and I have to start the message with my own coded identification so the Chief knows who is sending the message. If we really wanted to be tricky, we could change to another letter in mid-message and really confuse somebody" said Scott.

"You learn this stuff in the Army?" asked Frank.

"Of course. The Army can be real good at some of this kind of stuff," laughed Scott.

"Well, while you do all that writing, I'm gonna go get us a couple of rabbits for dinner," said Schuster, pulling his rifle out of its scabbard. "I got just enough time before it gets dark."

Scott worked quickly coding his message, barely noticing three shots in the distance, and was just finishing when Schuster returned with three freshly gutted and skinned rabbits. Scott said, "I'm glad you didn't decide to shoot me back at the ranch. Three shots, three rabbits is pretty good."

"And don't forget it," said the older man.

"My mouth is watering already," replied Scott.

"Well, you don't get any until you finish your chores, young man," growled Schuster.

"Yes, pa," replied Scott as he began tapping out the message.

After dinner, Schuster rolled himself a cigarette while Scott drank the last of the coffee. "How long before we get a message back?" Schuster asked.

"Probably sometime in the morning. The Chief has to contact a Federal Judge, then go through the proper channels in the Army, and then he usually deals direct with the Fort Commander," answered Scott. "With any luck, we will have this whole thing finished in a day or two."

"I still think it would have been better to just sneak down there and arrest those outlaws," complained Schuster.

"Sometimes I think you're right," said Scott, settling into his sleeping bag and closing his eyes.

CHAPTER 33

When the Chief got to his office in the morning, there was already a telegram on his desk. He quickly sliced the envelope open and realized it was a coded message from Will. The Chief went to his safe, spun the dial to the combination, and removed a wheel code device with Will's name on it.

It took the Chief thirty minutes to decode the message. With a muttered curse, he loudly called to Doris, "Get Donnally and Bell up here right away."

While waiting for the two operatives, the Chief mulled over the message, weighing different possibilities.

When Donnally and Bell got to the Chief's office, Doris was pointing them in before they could even greet her.

"Here is the latest from Will," said the Chief, handing over the decoded telegram.

After scanning the message, the pair looked up. "At least Miguel is alive," said Eddie.

"Darn lucky," said the Chief. "Will has obviously found the plant site, and the two missing brothers are doing the work."

"I wonder who the civilian is that's helping Will?" asked Bell.

"Sounds like it's someone who knows the area, given the plant's apparent somewhat remote location," said Donnally.

"I've been sitting here trying to figure out this whole scheme of Maddox's," mused the Chief. "Unfortunately, it beats the heck out of me."

"I'd like to tell you that me and John have figured something out, but we are in the same fix. No real reasonable plan jumps out at us either," said Eddie.

"Maybe they are going to bring it back East under cover of Maddox and Stang's trip. But, why set up the plant way the heck out there?" asked Bell rhetorically.

"I'm leaving day after tomorrow with those two weasels. I've changed my mind. I want you two to go home and get packed and head for Denver on the next available train. Don't let anyone know where you are going. You can check in with the Denver office once you get there. Stay at the Brown Palace and be ready to go at a moment's notice. If Joe Walker is in the office, brief him, and then let him make arrangements for the three of you to get to Silver Creek or wherever. I'll telegraph you right at the Brown Palace," instructed the Chief.

"What is this celebration you are going out for?" asked Eddie.

"The BEP is sending $20 million in Monroe $100s out to Silver Creek and bringing back 20 million in gold bars," replied the Chief. "It's celebrating all the gold that has been mined in that area."

"If they have all that gold there, why is the place called Silver Creek?" asked Bell.

"It's one of those crazy mining stories that happens to be true," answered the Chief. "I had the same question. The first miners in the area discovered silver. There was a minor boom, and they called the town that sprang up Silver Creek. As the boom was winding down, some tenderfoot Easterner, who didn't know what he was doing, stumbled across what he thought was an interesting rock. He took it in to the assay office to see what it was, and it was a chunk of gold the size of your fist. Then the boom was really on!"

"How did you know about that, Chief?" asked Eddie.

"I actually had the same question and put Doris on it. She had all the info within an hour," laughed the Chief.

"What about the Army, Chief? Are you going to bring them in?" asked Bell.

"I'm going over and talk to the Secretary as soon as you two leave. I'll see what detachment they have available and how quick they can get to the area," replied the Chief. "I'm not telling him about our suspects. We are the only three that know. I expect Will suspects someone here, but I doubt he suspects it's the Secretary. If you two have any great ideas, track me down day or night," added the Chief, dismissing them with the usual wave of his hand.

Eddie turned just as he got to the door. "By the way, we haven't heard back from those supply house inquiries, but I don't guess it matters now," said Eddie.

The Chief wasn't kept waiting at the Secretary of the Army's Office even though he didn't have an appointment. The two men greeted each other warmly, but the Secretary was surprised at the Chief's unscheduled appearance. "Listen Jamieson," said the Chief. "I'm not going to beat around the bush. We need your help once again. I've got an operative in Colorado who has located a counterfeit plant, and he needs help. His partner survived an ambush and he's getting some civilian help, but he is really out on a limb."

"Since it's Colorado, I'm assuming it's Will Scott," said Jamieson.

"It is," said the Chief. "But I'm going to have to ask you to trust me and not go through channels like we normally do."

"I see," said the Secretary. "Since I've never had this kind of request from you, I'll handle it as privately as I can. We have a detachment that's guarding a shipment of currency going to Silver Creek, Colorado later this week. They are picking up a large gold shipment and taking it to Denver."

"That's great," said the Chief.

"Unfortunately, they will be tied up with that for about the next ten days," said the Secretary, frowning. "Colonel Wilcox is in charge, and I know he's worked with your operatives several times. I also know he will keep his mouth shut when he gets a message from me outside of channels. I can instruct him however you want. Is that soon enough?"

"Actually, I'm going to that Celebration myself," said the Chief. "If you just have him contact me there, it would be perfect."

"You know, when this case is over, you're going to have to come clean over whiskey and cigars," laughed the Secretary.

"You're on," said the Chief, standing to leave. As he left, the Chief thought to himself: if you only knew. You should act like we never had this conversation.

When he got back to his office, the Chief composed a coded message to Will and asked Doris to send it right away. "Lord, what a way to spend a morning," he murmured to himself.

CHAPTER 34

It was mid-morning before a telegraph operator up the line began relaying the return coded message to Scott. It was a long message that had him frowning even before he began the decoding work.

"What's the matter?" asked Schuster.

"I don't like the way this looks. It's way too long for a regular message. Usually it's just directions on when and where to rendezvous with the Army," replied Scott.

He worked quickly on the decoding, but before he was half done, he was swearing to himself.

"The Chief says the Army Commander is unable to meet us for at least a week. The entire detachment is being used to transport and guard a shipment of twenty million dollars," explained Scott.

"That's going to Silver Creek for the celebration," exclaimed Schuster.

"Celebration at Silver Creek?" queried Scott.

"Yeah, they've refined twenty million in gold bars, and they're sending it to Washington in exchange for twenty million in greenbacks," answered Schuster. "I'm surprised you haven't heard about it."

"Why aren't they using the banking system for this?" asked Scott, a little embarrassed.

"Well, the boom actually started twenty years ago, and they're putting on this humdinger celebration to commemorate the boom and all that gold," replied Schuster.

Scott grunted to himself and continued to work on decoding the message.

"The Chief wants us to meet him at Silver Creek. No more of the counterfeit has turned up anywhere, and he wants to go with us to arrest these hombres," said Scott. "He is going to use the money shipment and the celebration as a reason for leaving D.C."

"There's gonna be all kind of famous fellas at this celebration—the Governor, Senator Jackson, as well as that Secretary of the Treasury fella," said Schuster.

"The Chief doesn't want anyone to know I'm around town. He says the only people who know we've located the counterfeiters out here are him and the Army Commander. He says he has some suspects himself that we can talk over together when I see him," said Scott.

"Are we heading for Silver Creek?" asked Frank.

"No, let's ride for the ranch. Nothing is going to happen until after the Celebration," answered Scott. "In addition, I want to go over all the facts with Miguel and see if we can make some sense out of everything we know."

"I know Lisa was planning on going to the celebration even before you showed up," answered Frank. "You won't be going alone."

Scott sent a straight message, coded but short, telling the Chief he understood the message and would comply. They quickly broke camp, mounted up and began to push toward the ranch.

"What are you gonna tell Lisa about all this?" asked Schuster, bringing up the sore subject again.

"I'm gonna tell her the truth about me and what I do for work. I just hope it won't make her decide to run me off," replied Scott.

"I don't know what she's gonna say about all this, but I'm figuring she's looking to brand you, no matter what," laughed the older man. "But let her blow off the steam that's been building ever since we left."

CHAPTER 35

Scott reddened and pushed his horse into a ground-eating lope. They got back to the ranch just after dark. Everybody but Miguel was at the kitchen table when they clattered up to the back door. Lisa was the first one out the door and was in Will's arms before both his feet were on the ground. She gave him a hug and a kiss that left him red-faced and breathless.

"I'm really glad you're back," she breathed, as her brothers came out to welcome them back.

"I'll take care of the horses," exclaimed Carl, grabbing both sets of reins and leading the horses toward the barn.

"You'd think we'd been gone a year instead of, what, four days," laughed Schuster.

"How's Miguel doing?" asked Will, trying to hide his discomfort and embarrassment.

"He's doing great. He's been able to walk a few steps, and he's been eating like a horse," replied Lisa.

"How was your trip?" asked Albert. "I don't see any bags of gold dust."

"It was good. I can't remember when I accomplished so much in so short a time," laughed Schuster, before Will could reply, and ignoring Albert's question.

The group moved into the kitchen for coffee and the rest of their supper. Louisa had already set two extra plates by the time they got inside. "Let me run up to visit Miguel quickly before I eat," said Will, disengaging himself from Lisa's arm and heading for Miguel's room.

He gave a light knock, then stuck his head inside and was surprised to find Miguel sitting in a chair looking at a newspaper.

"I don't know why you're looking at that. You and I both know you can't read English," laughed Will, knowing full well Miguel could read every word.

"I don't know how you returned without me to help you," replied Miguel.

Will shook his friend's hand and began to briefly summarize the results of his journey.

"I'll come back after supper and we can plan what to do next," said Will.

"I have had many conversations with Lisa, mi amigo, and it is very difficult. She asks many questions and is a savvy señorita," said Miguel.

"I'm planning on telling her the truth about us and what we do," replied Scott.

"Thank goodness. Sometimes only the truth will satisfy," laughed Miguel. "She already thinks me a big liar, I suspect. The next step will probably be torture."

"I'll be back later. Glad you're recovering," said Scott, as he headed for the supper table.

Everyone else was nearly finished eating when Scott walked into the kitchen. Lisa jumped up and fixed him a plate and a cup of coffee.

"We've been pestering Uncle Frank about your mining claim and everything," exclaimed Lisa, giving him a look full of suspicion.

"Darn nosy bunch, if you ask me," grumbled Schuster, rolling his eyes at Scott.

"Well, I guess they got a right to be nosy what with all the commotion my partner and I have caused around here," said Scott. "First off, I guess I ought to apologize to everybody about not telling you the entire truth about me and Miguel. We're not prospectors at all. I probably know less about mining than anybody here."

"I don't understand," interrupted Lisa, looking back and forth with a scowl at Scott and Schuster. "But I'm not surprised."

"You see," said Scott, fishing his badge and commission book out of a vest pocket and displaying it, "Miguel and I work for the United States government, actually the Secret Service Division of the Treasury Department. We were out here on the trail of people who are making some very dangerous counterfeit money. They are the ones who nearly killed Miguel, and your Uncle Frank has been helping me find their headquarters," explained Will.

"Did you really find 'em?" asked Carl excitedly.

"Yeah, we did," replied Schuster. "Why don't you boys come on out to the parlor and I'll spin the whole yarn out to you."

Louisa quickly added, "I'll see to Miguel."

They left Lisa and Will alone in the kitchen with their coffee and the warm cooking stove.

"You didn't have to lie to me, you know," said Lisa, a hurt expression showing in her eyes.

"I didn't lie so awful much. I mostly just told you half-truths," mumbled Scott.

"Why don't you just start at the beginning, Mr. Will Scott, or whatever your name is, and I'll do the deciding about how big a liar you are," Lisa replied, her lips set in a firm line.

So Will Scott told her his life story. He began with all about growing up with the family horses and about going off to military school. He spoke proudly of his brother, his sister-in-law and his two nieces. He again told her about his shortened military career and how sick it made him over the military's treatment and killing of helpless Indians. This time he included more details and confessed his guilt feelings. He related his career with the Secret Service and all the operatives he and Miguel had worked with over the past several years. Before he was done, she was holding his hand and smiling at the little quirks in his stories.

Occasionally, he would get up and put a little wood in the kitchen stove. No one in the family came in, and it was like they were in their own little cocoon.

For Will Scott, it was like a great burden being lifted off his soul, and as Lisa became more receptive, Will spoke more about his feelings and desires.

Lisa told him how much she loved the ranch and the horses, despite all the work. She told him about going to school back East, mostly because of her mother. He particularly liked her story about the first big social after she got to Boston. Her mother had bought her a beautiful dress, and all the parents were around the edges of the ballroom watching all the young people dance and mingle. She laughed when she related how an upperclassman who had been drinking whispered something in her ear about going out back and acting like farm animals. Much to his surprise, her reply was a quick punch to his nose, which resulted in a nose bleed and him being helped away by his friends.

"Not very lady like," Will laughingly added.

She told him about how much her father had loved nature and the outdoors, as well as his utter devotion to her mother. She smiled when she related how her socialite mother had left all that behind for her father, a decision she said in later years was the smartest thing she ever did. Lisa cried a little relating again how the one died basically because one couldn't live without the other.

Emotions pent up for years came tumbling out of both and they felt the warm glow of two kindred, formerly solitary souls, coming together. When they were finally done, Lisa was sitting in his lap with her head in the crook of his neck. Emotionally spent, they clung to each other while the glowing embers slowly turned to grey ash and the dark night lightened to an early dawn.

Both were shocked when Louisa knocked. "You two need to go do whatever. I've got a breakfast to get ready," she said. They had talked for hours without even realizing it. Each stood up, stretched, and walked out of the kitchen holding hands. Louisa smiled, shook her head, and went to cooking, humming a Mexican love song.

CHAPTER 36

The next morning, Eddie Donnally and John Bell caught the express train headed West. The express train only stopped in the bigger cities, like Cincinnati, St. Louis, and Chicago. They would change trains in Chicago to arrive in Denver. The trip would take almost three days and almost drove the pair crazy. They paced from one end of the train to the other and occasionally played cards with some of their fellow travelers. They read and re-read the latest issues of National Geographic, American Rifleman and Field and Stream, as well as newspapers, along the way. Even though they were for the most part city guys, inactivity was not their strong suit.

After arriving in Denver, they checked into the Brown Palace and then made their way to the Denver Office, located in the Federal Courthouse, Post Office Building. As they entered the office, they spied Joseph Walker, the Operative-in-Charge of the office.[5]

"Howdy, Joe," said Eddie.

Walker's mouth dropped open. "What!" he exclaimed.

"Isn't that what they say out here?" John Bell asked laughingly.

"Yeah, that's what they say," said Walker. "But not usually

---

[5] Author's Note: The real Joseph A. Walker, Operative-in-Charge of the Denver Field Office, was murdered in 1907, while investigating a complex land swindle in Durango, Colorado. His killers were identified, but no one was ever convicted of the crime.

with a New York accent." He frowned. "This is not good news when you two show up with no warning."

Eddie noticed a young female secretary. "Top of the morning ma'am," he said, tipping his hat.

"Miss Jenkins, meet two of Washington's finest operatives," said Walker. "Eddie Donnally and John Bell. You should avoid any social contact with either one, as they are no-count, womanizing, city fellas," added Walker.

"Fortunately, I'm engaged to a Deputy U.S. Marshall, so I think I'll be safe," answered Miss Jenkins, smiling.

"What a pity," said Eddie, throwing up his hands.

Walker gestured them into an inner office. "Okay, what gives?" asked Walker.

Donnally and Bell filled Walker in on the entire case, including the Chief's arrival in Silver Creek.

"We're at the Brown Palace, and the Chief wants us and you ready to go at a moment's notice," advised Eddie.

"How far is Silver Creek?" asked Bell.

"It's just a couple of hours by train, but the regular train only goes up there three times a week," said Walker. "But the mining companies have private trains running up there every day, so we can catch one of those if we need to. I know all the mine security guys. We could get some fast horses hired up," he added, barely suppressing a laugh.

"It's never a good idea to mess with an Irishman, Joseph. A leprechaun will bring you bad luck," snapped Eddie. While Donnally and Bell had ridden horses, it was something neither one enjoyed.

"This case is really something," said Walker. "You know I don't doubt anything you fellas say, but we are way short of hard evidence, especially when two of the suspects are members of the President's Cabinet. Even if we don't arrest them, they are bound to figure we know the story."

"You're right," chorused Bell and Donnally.

"We'll get the counterfeit plant, but if we don't get them, there will be the dickens to pay," said Bell.

"All we can do is wait," said Walker. "I know where you guys are staying, and here's my address. Soon as we hear something, we can get going."

Bell and Donnally left the office, with Eddie giving Miss Jenkins a beaming smile while shaking his head.

CHAPTER 37

James "Jimmy" Hauptman was sweating as he worked the cantilever handle that dropped the razor sharp blade on the sheets of counterfeit currency. He was a skilled pressman and could operate and maintain a platen press with the best around. When he worked at the Bureau of Engraving and Printing in Washington, he had a helper to change the plates, load and unload the stacks of paper and do the cutting. Out here in the wilderness, he had to do everything. The camp cook, while not bad at cooking, was just a strong back when it came to the printing operation.

His older brother, Franz, was a skilled engraver, and when he had been employed by the Bureau of Engraving and Printing, he, too, had been provided assistants. The two brothers were very skilled, and while they were proud of their skill, they were extremely greedy. The German-speaking Swiss brothers wanted more of the American dream, and they wanted it right away. Despite having only been in America for three years and having decent paying government jobs, they decided to improve their lot in life by stealing.

They concocted a simple but successful scheme. Jimmy worked the presses where the money was printed and was therefore carefully watched anytime he left the Bureau of Engraving and Printing building. His brother Franz, the engraver, had no contact with the part of the building where the currency was actually printed and stored. He only worked on the big, heavy printing plates that nobody could put under their coat and walk out with. The two brothers met in the common lunch room every day, each with a black lunch box. During the morning, Jimmy would carefully pinch bills during the cutting process and hide them in his lunch box. At lunch time, they ate their packed lunches and easily exchanged lunch boxes. This went on for 18 months. Jimmy's lunch box, along with those of the other printing area employees, was occasionally searched by the BEP police guards. Franz was never even given a second look, much less a search, since he exited from a different part of the big building. The brothers were slick, but not nearly as slick as they thought. Eventually, one of the supervisors noticed that some of the counts kept coming up a little short here and there. Some surreptitious observation from the hidden catwalks throughout the building soon identified the brothers and their little scheme. It wasn't the first time an employee had stolen or tried to steal from the BEP.

Reports were written, and eventually the reports went to the Secretary of the Treasury so he could authorize the arrest of the two brothers. While the BEP hated thieves, the bureau equally hated any publicity or any general public knowledge about internal thefts. The Secretary of the Treasury—in this case, Alvin T. Maddox—was the ultimate authority.

For Maddox, it was the ultimate gift. He had a burning desire to steal from the government, but he needed people from the BEP to accomplish his scheme. The problem he faced was finding BEP employees he could corrupt. While his scheme was not really formed, a skilled plate engraver and a printer finally allowed him to formulate a detailed plan. Being the Secretary, he knew of the scheduled shipment of twenty million dollars to

Colorado. Since he and his cousin, Andrew, were running land and mining swindles in that area, he had been thinking of anything he could do to get at that 20 million dollars. Maddox, knowing he could count on his cousin, quickly concocted a plan to have the Hauptmans print 20 million in counterfeit and engineer a substitution. Andrew had come to Washington as quick as he could with his own thug, Simpkins. Maddox briefed his cousin on what he wanted him to do. Andrew and Simpkins, using ID's obtained by the Secretary, barged in on the brothers in their rented rooms and quickly handcuffed them. The almost 20 thousand dollars stolen from the BEP was hidden under loose boards beneath a clothes dresser. Normally, it would have been a good hiding place, but crooks like Andrew and Simpkins found the stash within 20 minutes. Jimmy had been indignant at first, but after Simpkins punched him in the stomach and then backhanded his face, his older and weaker brother, Franz, was crying like a baby.

The two thugs told them it was leave with them for a special job for an important person or go the next morning with the BEP police. The brothers packed a suitcase each and left with the two men, who had pocketed their money. By midnight, the four men were on a train to Chicago. While the two brothers were not happy, they both knew in their hearts that their new "partners" would gladly hurt or kill them if they didn't go along.

CHAPTER 38

O n the trip West, the four men were inseparable. The man who said his name was Andrew White was obviously in charge, and he instructed them in what they would be doing in the partnership. He was a very slick talker. Jimmy knew he and his brother were making a pact with the devil, but what choice did they have? White told them his syndicate wanted them to print 20 million dollars in Monroe $100 bills. The brothers had four weeks to complete the job, and for their efforts, they would receive a million dollars in genuine currency. White also told the brothers they could go to San Francisco and live like kings on their million dollars.

The brothers gave Andrew White a list of the printing equipment and supplies they would need, and several times on the way to Chicago, he sent telegrams. Jimmy and Franz were both amazed that when they arrived in Chicago, Andrew White met a freight wagon and paid to have a brand new platen press like Jimmy wanted loaded on the train. The brothers had entered America in Baltimore and had never ventured outside the Baltimore and Washington area. This train trip had them in awe at the sheer size of America.

In St. Louis, two more wagons met the train and White again paid to have supplies loaded. Jimmy noticed that the supplies were what he and Franz had listed but they came from several different suppliers. He also noticed that White paid everyone in cash, and while they were supposed to be partners, Jimmy was pretty sure the cash was the money that he and his brother had so carefully stolen from the BEP. They had eventually ended up at this mining site, which to the brothers, born and raised in the city, seemed to be the end of the earth. Every few days, a wagon or two would appear with supplies. Originally, there had been two men with them at the site, the cook and a surly man named Douglas. They all called the cook "Cookie", and the brothers never inquired about his real name. The brothers didn't have time for anything but getting to work on their task. Four weeks was not long for what they had to do, so all they did was eat, sleep and work. Shortly after they began printing some finished bills, Douglas had ridden the only horse out, saying he was going to town. Andrew White and Simpkins, along with a man named Fredericks, usually showed up with the supply wagons and made sure the drivers unloaded the wagons and left without seeing either the brothers or the money they were making. Andrew White would examine the counterfeit, and Jimmy and Franz were encouraged by White's praise of their work. The money was not perfect, but Jimmy and Franz knew it was pretty darned good.

"Franz," Jimmy called, raising his voice to be heard over the steam engine and the cutter, "help me get another load lined up."

Franz got up off a cot in the corner and put on his thick glasses. "What is the count now, Jimmy?"

"We are at nineteen five now and we have two more days," said Jimmy.

The brothers spoke with German accents, but their English understanding was excellent. For three years, they had tried to speak only English and resorted to German only with each other when they didn't want anyone to understand their conversation.

Speaking in German, Franz asked Jimmy, for what seemed like the thousandth time, "Jimmy, how do you think this will turn out?"

Answering in German, the same way he always did, Jimmy said, "Franz, what choice do we have? Either we are partners like Andrew says or we are captives. No matter which, we have to print this money and hope for the best."

Franz said, "Okay," and loaded another stack of counterfeit currency sheets on the cutting table. "Jimmy," asked Franz, "what is the first thing you are going to do when we get to San Francisco?"

"I'm going to find me the strongest beer in town and a huge plate of blood sausages," laughed Jimmy.

"I've already etched enough plates and reset the numbering wheels, so we will be finished sometime tomorrow," said Franz.

"Excellent, maybe we will get a bonus for finishing early," said Jimmy, arching his eyebrows.

CHAPTER 39

As Scott and Lisa left the kitchen and started down the bedroom wing hall, they looked at each other and fireworks went off. He was kissing her, she was kissing him, and they were in an embrace as close as two people could be. Neither even came close to noticing Carl as he came out of his bedroom.

"Excuse me," stammered Carl, looking down, turning red and suppressing a huge grin all at the same time.

Lisa and Will stepped apart to let Carl pass. "I guess I had better go freshen up for breakfast," said Lisa.

"Me, too," replied Will. "I've got to talk to Miguel and then I'll meet you in the kitchen."

Will gave a soft knock, and Miguel answered, "Come in, mi amigo." One look at Will's face and Miguel asked, assuming a priestly pose, "Is there something wrong, my son?"

"Shut up," said Will, shaking his head. "Nothing is wrong, except I've found someone besides you to spend my whole life with, in the middle of the biggest and probably most dangerous case we've ever worked."

"By that, your revelations to Lisa must have gone muy bien," answered Miguel.

"Revelations? What have you been doing, reading the dictionary up here?" growled Will.

"Unlike you, El Jefe," answered Miguel, "I have been reading the newspaper and have an idea about our case."

"Go ahead. I have to admit this case has not entered my mind in the past few hours," said Will sheepishly.

"Were los hombres you saw at the mining site printing a lot of money?" asked Miguel.

"Way more than we've ever seen before, and they've got a lot of money invested in equipment and supplies," answered Scott, now focusing fully back on the case. "They were using belt driven equipment, which I've never seen except in a commercial print shop."

"Lying around here, it made me muy curiosa about what they could do with all this counterfeit money," mused Miguel. "I could not think of anything until this," Miguel said, picking up the newspaper and pointing to an article headlined, "20 million in greenbacks to appear at Celebration in Silver Creek."

"Of course," Will exclaimed. "It all makes sense now. Schuster told me about the Celebration. Somehow they are planning to swap the counterfeit they are making out here with the genuine 20 million coming from Washington. It's why they are making so much at one time. They are not going to sell it off in batches; they are going to use it all at once."

"It all makes sense to me, too, amigo, especially since we know someone in Washington is involved in this," said Miguel.

"That someone is bound to be coming out for this. No criminal, especially one as smart as this one, will trust all that money to other crooks," exclaimed Will.

"It says the Governor, the U.S. Senator, and it also lists the Secretary of the Interior and the Secretary of the Treasury," answered Miguel. "I can no believe it is someone such as this."

Scott sat back in his armchair, and thinking out loud he said, "You know, when I went back to D.C., the Chief said only he, the Secretary and the Chief Engraver knew about the counterfeit. Like you, even though we knew someone leaked the information about us, I would never have suspected the Secretary. I was really stupid about this. I was so busy looking forward; I never took the time to step back and really see the answer. But, you know, we really have nothing to connect the Secretary to any of these people out here."

"Don't blame yourself. This is muy grande," exclaimed Miguel. "Not even the dime store book man would ever write up something like this!"

"I think the Chief is wise to some of this, Miguel. He sent me a message that he was coming to Silver Creek and to meet him there," explained Will. "I can't wait to hear what he has uncovered in Washington."

"I no like this, Will. You are going there alone. Even with the Chief there, you are certain to be outnumbered. We know these crooks are, how you say, worst of the worst," exclaimed Miguel. He had a stricken look on his face and was as close to tears as Will had ever seen him.

At that moment, Lisa stuck her head in the door and asked, "Are you coming down to breakfast or are you waiting for lunch?"

Giving his best friend's arm a squeeze, he said, "I'll be back later and we will all come up with some kind of plan."

"Take good care of him señorita," Miguel said to their backs as they went toward the bedroom door.

"Hey, don't think you are off the hook, mister, just because you have a couple of bullet holes. I owe you some aggravation," replied Lisa, giving him a stern look over her shoulder. The stern look was tempered with a slight smile.

When they got to the kitchen, Will realized that everyone was waiting on him and the big breakfast had been getting cold.

"I'm sorry," said Will. "Miguel and I have been going over all we know, and we think we know the counterfeiters' plan. We believe their goal is to exchange 20 million in counterfeit for the 20 million in genuine currency that is being shipped out for the Celebration."

"Won't that be difficult with all the guards, not to mention that's a lot of money?" asked Albert.

"The truth is 20 million dollars in Monroe $100 notes doesn't take up much space, probably less than half of a freight wagon," replied Will. "We suspect that the head of this thing is probably the Secretary of the Treasury. Only very few people in Washington ever knew about this case, and he would be one of the few people who could manage this affair without too many helpers. Miguel and I just don't know how he is connected to the people out here. It could actually be someone else."

"I can't believe somebody that important could be behind all this," said Lisa, shaking her head.

Schuster snorted, "Politicians are capable of anything."

"The main people out West would be Andrew White and the two I think tried to kill Miguel, Frederick and Simpkins," said Will. "To be successful, you have to keep the number of people involved as small as possible." He then added, "Normally, like I explained to Frank, we would notify the Chief and arrange to have the Army help us round this bunch up. But we've got to get the men behind this operation. If we are right, and I think we are, this is so much more than the normal counterfeit case. The two men doing the printing at that old mining site are just hired hands. I suspect, given the ruthlessness we've seen so far, those two fellas will be lucky to be alive after their work is finished."

"I'll go to Silver Creek to meet up with the Chief and see if we can get this whole crowd arrested," continued Will.

Lisa held up her hand in a stop motion and held it up with such an intense glare that Will sat back.

"First, we have been having a family meeting while you were doing your talking with Miguel, and you are not going anywhere without all of us. There is no way we are letting you go alone. It is way too dangerous even for you. We were planning on going to the Celebration anyway," said Lisa.

Will started to speak, but Frank cut him off. "Son, this matter is settled, so you might as well go ahead with what you need us to do."

"I guess I know when to surrender," said Will gravely, "but everyone should remember how Miguel was almost killed and how dangerous these people are. I couldn't live with myself if something happened to any of you," Will continued, staring straight at Lisa. "Exactly how long will it take to get to Silver Creek?" asked Will.

"It will take about a day and a half by regular and mining roads, driving a wagon, maybe a little longer. But definitely, not much more than a day and a full afternoon," replied Frank. "Maybe only one day in an empty wagon, assuming there are no washouts to the road and you don't mind traveling at night."

"By riding horses and using trails Uncle Frank and I know, we can be there in one long day," added Lisa.

"How well are you folks known in Silver Creek?" asked Will.

"All the old-timers know us," piped in Schuster and Albert

in unison.

"Lisa's been sparked by a bunch of fellas over there," blurted Carl, causing Lisa to blush bright red and everybody else, including Will, to laugh.

"As I was saying," barked Schuster, stopping the laughter, "everyone will notice and start gossiping if they see you and Lisa together."

"It's important that nobody notice me much; I want to be just another ranch hand in town for the Celebration," said Will.

"We'll be staying at the Stagecoach Hotel near the center of town," said Lisa. "We can get an extra room and you can come up the back stairs at night. That way, nobody will know where you're staying. Besides, it's the best hotel in town and the Secretary, your Chief and the Army Commander are sure to be staying there."

"Are you sure you can get rooms there?" asked Will. "There's sure to be a heap of folks in town."

"Oh, don't worry," said Carl, "Harry Cox, the owner, is sweet on Lisa, and he sent word last week that he had rooms reserved for us."

The sudden silence following Carl's reply was broken by Lisa's laughter. "If there's anything you don't know about me, Will, just ask my brother. He seems to be an expert on all my business."

"Please understand that you can't tell anyone about me," requested Scott. "There are almost certainly people involved in this scheme that we know nothing about. You must act like you're there for the celebration and I'm just a hired hand. Using Army personnel, we can make the arrests and put an end to this thing," advised Will. "The hard part will be getting enough evidence to arrest the Secretary if he's the guilty one.   He is going to be in the background pulling strings.   He's not the kind to get his hands dirty," continued Will.

"Well, let's get going, you lazy no counts," growled Schuster, "We've got a week's worth of chores to do before we go to town."

They all spent the rest of the week preparing for the trip, and mainly preparing the ranch to maintain itself during the time they were away.   In the late afternoon, the day before they were to leave, Miguel and Will sat on the front porch and went over everything in the case again from the beginning.

"You need to be careful, mi amigo . . . you no have me there to cover you.   That old man Schuster, he pretty good, but he no Mexicano," grinned Miguel.

Scott helped Miguel into the kitchen for supper, where the whole family was buzzing like bees about the upcoming trip to town.   Carl and Albert reluctantly agreed to drive a wagon to town so they could bring back supplies to the ranch.   The wagon couldn't negotiate some of the shortcut trails, so it would take them longer than they wanted to get there.   Will and Lisa didn't talk much during supper, and afterward, they were busy getting things ready for the trail.   But before turning in, they ended up alone in the kitchen together.

"You know you better be careful in Silver Creek, Mr. Will Scott," said Lisa, giving his hand a squeeze.   "I've got big plans for you afterward," she added.

"Don't worry, I know now I've got a place to come home to," said Scott, pulling her close and giving her a long slow kiss.

"You're going to make us do something indecent here in the kitchen," laughed Lisa.

Scott laughed with her as Louisa came shuffling into the kitchen.

"Goodnight," Lisa beamed as she left the kitchen, leaving behind a frustrated Will Scott. They both knew their relationship would have to wait until his case was finished, but neither one liked it.

CHAPTER 40

They were all up that morning before dawn. The horses could sense the excitement and anticipation as they were being saddled or harnessed to the wagon. Miguel made it out to the porch and waved goodbye as the riders and wagon rode out of the yard. The group rode together for an hour before they reached the side trail that would take the horses out of the valley and over the ridge.

"We'll have you boys a steak dinner ready whenever you get to the hotel," promised Schuster.

"With a big slice of apple pie," laughed Carl.

Lisa got off her horse and gave them both motherly hugs. "Be careful," she admonished. After shaking hands with Will, the wagon carrying the brothers rolled on while the horses started up the trail.

The trail was not really wide enough to ride more than two abreast, so conversation was limited to Lisa or Schuster telling Will about landmarks or natural features they were passing. Around midday, they stopped by a cascading stream and watered the horses. While Will tethered the horses to some low growing bushes so they could snatch their fill of grass, Lisa unwrapped some thick slices of meat and bread Louisa had packed.

"What do you think of this shortcut so far?" asked Schuster.

"It reminds me of our last trip, but the company is better," said Scott, winking at Lisa. "What's this place called?"

"It really doesn't have a name," replied Lisa, "at least not an English name. There are some Indian cliff ruins a little ways east. Dad probably noted some Indian name in his journals, but I don't remember it."

"It's just as well," shrugged Will. "The Indian name is probably better than any English name."

"No doubt," said Schuster. "The Indians lived with the land, so the names meant something. The white man just goes right over it, most not ever noticing."

"You boys are downright gloomy. C'mon, we're going to town for a celebration, not a funeral," exclaimed Lisa.

"Let's ride," grumbled Schuster.

The last few miles of the trip were mostly flat, and Schuster led them in some noisy renditions of a few well-known cattle drive songs. They cantered into town just as twilight arrived and were barely off their horses before the hotel man was down the steps and grabbing Lisa's hand.

"Hello, Lisa, it's wonderful to see you again," babbled Harry Cox. It was an obvious fact that Cox was enamored of Lisa. But they were items in contrast. Cox was dressed in the fanciest clothes this side of St. Louis, and from the toes of his city boots to the top of his perfectly combed head, a city slicker. As comfortable as Cox was in his garb, Lisa was just as comfortable in hers, and for Scott, she couldn't have looked better in a fancy ball gown. Although dusty from the long ride, she radiated an earthy outdoor aura.

Scott had prepared himself to ignore any of Lisa's suitors and carry on in his role as a hired drifter. Even though he didn't feel threatened by Cox, he could feel his neck redden as he overheard the city slicker's compliments and heard Lisa's laughter. Schuster introduced them, but Cox didn't give Scott a second glance. He was too busy escorting Lisa to the front desk. The lobby was crowded with people of all types, ranchers to mining magnates, and everything in-between. Several spoke to Schuster and nodded to Scott, but no one took any interest in what was obviously just another hired hand.

Schuster signed the hotel register for both he and Will. Cox made a big show of inviting them all to supper in the hotel dining room. Lisa and Schuster accepted, while Will declined, saying he wanted to visit the saloon. Cox had a bellboy carry Lisa's light bag up to her room.

"I hope you have some celebration clothes, Lisa," said Cox.

"My brothers are coming with a wagon. I have something very special to wear," flirted Lisa.

Lisa stayed in the lobby with Henry Cox, while Frank and Will carried their own saddlebags upstairs.

After quietly giving Schuster a quick run-down of his plans, Will found the back stairs and headed for the saloon. On the way, he passed the livery stable where he noticed a corral full of cavalry horses, and nearby the supply wagons that accompany a troop on the move. He didn't need any directions to find the saloon; you could hear the noise a half block away. Will slipped inside easily and worked his way to a good vantage point at the end of the bar. The Army was there in full force on the first floor drinking, along with an assortment of working men in all shapes and sizes. There was a large overhanging balcony, and the people on that level were the ones that caught Will's attention. He couldn't just go upstairs, since he wasn't dressed right, and somewhere up there were men tasked with keeping the working class downstairs.

He noted the scattering of Army officers, but didn't recognize anyone. The ranchers tended to dress in a western style, while the bankers and mine owners tended to dress in the popular back East styles. There was a large table around which a lot of people were moving. The crowd finally parted a little and Will glimpsed the Chief. The sight made Will smile into his glass. The Chief was wearing a gray western style suit with a matching oversized Stetson. His brightly colored vest and matching string tie separated him from everyone else. There was a bright peacock feather in his hat band. The Chief was making social conversation with several ladies and what Will took to be politicians and bankers. Will worked his way to a line of sight observation point and was rewarded two beers later with a slight nod in his direction from the Chief. Will nursed his beer a little longer and then ambled his way out of the saloon and down the street toward the hotel. Instead of going straight there, however, he crossed the street and wound his way around before ending up in the hotel lobby. Satisfied that no one had noticed and followed him, Will went into the hotel restaurant for supper.

Lisa, Schuster, and the hotel dandy were just finishing their dinner, and Will tipped his hat on his way to a table. He retrieved a Denver newspaper from a nearby chair and waited for his food and the Chief. The food was decent, and just as he finished eating, he saw the Chief come through the front doors of the hotel. The Chief had a short conversation with the desk clerk and when he was sure no one was looking, flashed Will a three finger signal.

Will swallowed the last of his coffee.

"That'll be two bits, cowboy," said the waitress.

"And a bargain it was," replied Will, flashing a big smile. Will casually strolled out of the restaurant and headed up the hotel stairs. He stopped at the 1st floor landing and waited several minutes. Satisfied no one was following, he continued to the 3rd floor. Halfway down the hall, the Chief stuck his head out and then motioned Will in, quickly shutting the door.

"Good Lord, was I glad to see you!" exclaimed the Chief, giving Will a bear hug. "Miguel is not dead, is he?"

"No, he was hit bad, but he's recovering quickly," answered Will. "The bullets went through and he never even developed much of a fever. The angels were surely watching over him."

"Is he in the hotel here?" asked the Chief.

"No, he's staying at the Cataloochee Ranch. It belongs to the Butler family. His horse ran after the ambush and thankfully ended up on their doorstep. Miguel was hanging on, barely conscious," replied Will.

"What happened with the ambush? Were you followed or did someone recognize you?" queried Will's boss, quickly getting down to business.

"They were waiting for us, Chief. If I hadn't gone off to send the telegram, we would probably both be dead," answered Will.

The Chief's face molded into a deep frown. "You're saying that somebody back East knew about you two and somehow is in cahoots with these counterfeiters?"

"It's the only thing that makes sense. We were shot at in Leadville and they were waiting on the trail in set positions," answered Will.

"Do you have any idea who we're dealing with?" asked the Chief.

"I was able to locate the counterfeit plant site and three of the men involved are Andrew White, Al Fredericks and a really nasty fellow named Simpkins. I think Fredericks and Simpkins are the ones who did the shooting. The two printers I've never seen before, but they're definitely not Westerners. If I was guessing, I'd say they are from Europe and are new to America," relayed Scott.

"I assume as soon as this celebration is over, we're headed for this place with the Army to round these no-counts up!" exclaimed the Chief.

"I have a surprise for you. I don't think we'll need to. I think they'll be coming to us," said Scott.

"What do you mean?" asked the Chief.

"I mean, you just brought 20 million dollars in genuine currency here. The crook that could engineer a way to swap a bunch of counterfeit for some, if not all, of that genuine money would make himself a real healthy profit," informed Scott.

"You sure you didn't get thrown off your horse and hit your head? This would be the granddaddy of all schemes. I want to go through all of it from the beginning to now," instructed the Chief, pulling up a chair to the room's writing table.

So that's what they did, the Chief making notes and filling Scott in on what was happening in D.C. Scott related the whole story, including all the details about Lisa and her family. The Chief frowned at parts and smiled at others.

"This young lady seems pretty special," smiled the Chief.

"That's true," replied a reddening Scott.

"This Schuster seems like my kind of man. I look forward to meeting them," exclaimed the Chief. "But back to business. After I learned someone was after you and Miguel, I started some discreet investigating of my own," informed the Chief.

"There were only about half a dozen people in Washington who knew about you and Miguel being on a case out West. But there was only one person, the Secretary, who knew about the high quality of counterfeit and the timetable you and Miguel were operating on, not to mention the towns involved in the operation," he continued. "But we don't have any real hard evidence."

"It's still hard to believe the actual Secretary of the Treasury is behind this whole thing," said Scott.

"I didn't tell anyone except him about the counterfeit and the status of your investigation," replied the Chief.

"Isn't it more likely that it was someone in his office who told, or a friend or something?" wondered Scott aloud.

"I had the same thoughts and doubts, but he is the most logical one," replied the Chief. "I had your buddy, Eddie Donnally, dig into his background going back to his days at the university. The police knew his cousin, Andrew White, was conducting all kind of illegal activities, but they could never get the goods on him or the rest of his gang. They actually suspected our boss as being the brains behind things, but never developed any proof. In addition, another one suspected of being involved was William Stang, our wonderful Secretary of the Interior. He is also here, by the way."

"That Andrew White is the missing link for me, Chief," Scott said excitedly. "White was running that Two Aces Cattle and Land Company."

"Let's see," said the Chief. "We have Maddox at the top, then his cousin and probably Stang as the main underlings. Although, I suspect Maddox and White are probably equals. Stang strikes me as a follower, not a leader," continued the Chief.

"After them," said Will, "you have Al Fredericks and that Simpkins as the tough guys. From what I could see at their mine site, the printers and the cook are at the bottom of the pecking order."

"Those bottom three may already be dead. This bunch doesn't seem inclined to leave witnesses," said the Chief. "When they left New Haven, an Italian kid who used to do some strong arm work with White was found in the river."

"They obviously intend to swap their counterfeit notes for the new $20 million from D.C. The question is how and where?" asked Scott rhetorically.

"I've known the Army Commander in Charge, Colonel Wilcox, for years and am about positive he's not involved," said the Chief. "However, he told me that this Captain Fairchild, specifically in charge of the money detail, is new and was assigned out of D.C., which is unusual in itself. The commander said he hated to admit it, but he just doesn't like the man and can't really explain why. He has said nothing to anyone about a counterfeit raid after this celebration."

"I'm with you, Wilcox is solid. He's helped us before. The only thing we can do is watch and wait until they make their move," stated Scott.

"What kind of operational plan do you have in mind?" asked the Chief.

"Well, counting you, Schuster, Lisa, Carl, Albert and me, that's six sets of eyes and ears. You can keep an eye on the Secretary," advised Will, "actually, both of the Secretaries, if possible."

"When I started to suspect the Secretary, I sent Donnally and Bell to Denver," said the Chief. "I'll telegraph them first thing in the morning and get them up here, along with Joe Walker. The hotel owner is on the bank's Board of Directors," replied the Chief. "I met him this afternoon."

"Lisa and Schuster can keep an eye on him. Unfortunately, he's sweet on Lisa," groused Scott. "To be fair, I don't think this bunch has included anyone but their tight little group and I don't think he is involved."

Barely suppressing a grin, the Chief said, "Although I'm convinced about your idea, I still don't see how they're going to make the swap. The gold and the money are both locked in the bank right now. Nobody can just pull a wagon up to the back door and make the switch in the middle of the night, especially without help from the Army or someone in the bank, probably both."

"I know," said Scott. "It seems an impossible thing to accomplish, but as sure as I'm sitting here, I know that's what they intend. In addition, they have to do it without causing a big fuss and drawing any attention."

"Well, they only have three days to do it before the Celebration and exchange ceremony," said the Chief.

"It is going to be a long three days," replied Scott.

"I'll come here to your room every night at 10:00 and fill you in. I'll try to get Lisa here at 10:00 also, to tell you what any of the family may have noticed," continued Will, heading for the door.

"If for some reason you don't come or send someone, all bets are off. I'll turn out the Army and scour the town," replied the Chief.

"You and I both know it will be too late by then!" said Will, slipping out the door.

CHAPTER 41

It was a little after 4:00, and Miguel was sitting in the kitchen, drinking coffee with Louisa. He had been edgy and anxious ever since Will, Lisa and Frank had left that morning. He had hobbled out to see Torreon, using a cane Louisa gave him. It had been a strain, but he had made it without collapsing. Louisa had watched his every step from the kitchen window.

"You are one hard-headed Mexicano," she was saying as they heard a commotion in front of the window.

"Hola, mamacita," they heard.

Louisa squealed with pleasure. "It is my nephew from New Mexico," she said, rushing to the front door.

By the time Miguel pushed himself up and hobbled to the door, Louisa was hugging three Mexican vaqueros.

"Miguel, this is my nephew, Juan Velazco." Juan was obviously the oldest of the three. "And these are our cousins, Manuel and Diego."

"Mucho gusto," said Miguel, shaking hands with each man in turn. Miguel looked out the door and saw six horses tied to the hitching rail. Three had saddles, and three didn't.

"¿Qué pasó, Juan?" asked Louisa.

"El Jefe sent us with three mares he wants Señorita Lisa to breed. He says they are the best of the best," replied Juan.

If looks were any indication, thought Miguel, El Jefe was right. They were outstanding. "You niños go stable the horses, and I will make some fresh coffee," said Louisa.

"Maybe some sopapillas, mamacita," Juan practically begged. "It's been a long ride."

"We'll see," said Louisa, giving Miguel a wink.

Thirty minutes later, the four men were stuffed. While they ate the sweets, Miguel had told them the whole story of him and Will, the counterfeit case, and how everyone was in Silver Creek.

"Amigos," said Miguel. "I know you just finished a long ride, but how would you feel about a little further ride?"

Louisa dropped the spoon she had been holding and started speaking in rapid fire Spanish. "Miguel, you are not well enough to ride to Silver Creek. Lisa would have a fit and Señor Will would not like it either. Besides, it may be dangerous for these niños." She immediately realized her mistake. The vaqueros, all around 20 years old, began talking excitedly about the offer of a great adventure.

"I'm sorry, Louisa," said Miguel. "These outlaws are very dangerous, and I just can't wait here doing nothing. How long would it take us to get there?"

Louisa just glared at the four men. "I don't know the back trails Lisa, Will and Frank took. I always ride in the wagon when we go to town. If you left at first light and rode hard, you could be there probably in the early evening. But you would each have to be leading one extra horse so you could keep swapping off. No one horse could travel at that pace, which is something all of you well know. It will be a long and difficult ride," she finished, pointing the spoon at Miguel. "Especially for you."

"Amigos, I'll go upstairs and get some things together and

the four of you can talk it over. This is not your fight, and Louisa is right. It could be dangerous," said Miguel. "I've made up my mind to go. I have to."

"There is no need to talk," said Juan, looking at the two others. "This family is our family, and we will go where we are needed."

Louisa glared and said, "You hombres are muy loco, but if you are going no matter what, I will fix food for the ride. But this is how it will be. Miguel, you go upstairs and get in bed, and you do not move until dawn. I will bring supper up to you. Juan, you boys go pick five of Lisa's horses and get Miguel's horse, Torreon, and make sure they have plenty of food and water. You know how to get them ready. Now, all of you get out of my sight," she said, waving her spoon at all of them.

The vaqueros were up before dawn, saddling the horses and getting things ready. Just as dawn was breaking, the four men clattered away from the house, leaving Louisa standing on the front porch. "Vaya con Dios," she said out loud, expressing herself with the sign of the cross.

CHAPTER 42

After leaving the Chief, Will tiptoed down the hall and lightly tapped on Lisa's hotel room door. The door opened, and Lisa pulled him in and gave him a serious hug, while gently closing the door.

"See, I told you he would show up eventually," said Schuster, who was lounging in an over-stuffed chair.

Lisa took Will's hand and made him sit on the bed beside her. "Let's have it," she said.

"I just left the Chief, and based on what we know so far, we think the Secretary of the Treasury, along with a man named Andrew White, are the brains of this group. We still have no idea how they intend to swap the money. They almost have to have included someone from the bank and the Army detail to help them," informed Will. "In addition, the Secretary of the Interior is almost certainly involved. The Captain of the actual Army money detail is suspect. He is new and was assigned out of D.C."

"I met the bank President tonight at dinner. His name is Joshua Stanley," said Lisa. "You can't miss him; he's always wearing bright colored vests. Henry says he calls them his trademark."

"So, what do you need us to do?" asked Schuster.

"Just keep your eyes peeled for anything unusual, even though it might be someone you know," answered Will. "I'll go to the Chief's room, #325, every night at 10 p.m. to brief him on what I've been doing. Lisa, it would be good if you could be there, too, and let him know if the family has noticed anything. If either me or one of the family doesn't show, the Chief will turn out the Army detail and begin to scour the town," advised Will.

"We'll do our best to make it, unless one of Lisa's suitors delays her. Son, I'm not about to give you that kind of hug if I have to show up," laughed Schuster, breaking the tension.

"Just be careful. These are dangerous men and they will do anything to make their scheme successful," cautioned Will. "The amount of money involved is really beyond imagination. The Chief is sending for three operatives that are in Denver. They should be here day after tomorrow."

"Carl and Albert got here a little while ago," said Frank. "They kept going after dark and didn't stop for anything but to water the horses.   The two of them are out wandering around just keeping their eyes open."

"I think they set a record," laughed Lisa. "They were afraid they were going to miss something."

"Come on, Romeo. Let's get out of here. It won't arouse anyone's suspicions if they see you with me, but you alone anywhere near her room wouldn't be good," instructed Schuster.

Will stood up to go, with Lisa still holding his hand.

"You fools go ahead and kiss so we can get out of here," growled the old man, slightly turning away.

Will gave Lisa a deep kiss and a strong hug, and then he and Frank were gone.

CHAPTER 43

The next morning was a beautiful late spring mountain day. The sky was blue with big puffy clouds, yet not so hot as to be uncomfortable. The town was alive. The people in this part of the country had worked hard and were proud of what they had collectively achieved. There was a cattle auction set up on the outskirts of town, along with side shows and acrobats. The Chief took all this in as he made his way to the Western Union Office.

"I need to send a message to some friends at the Brown Palace in Denver, young man," advised The Chief.

The young clerk practically stood at attention. "The wire is pretty busy, Chief, but I'll get it out first thing."

"It's going to a Mr. Edward Donnally," said the Chief. "Here's what I would like it to say." He handed the clerk the written message. "And, son, tell no one what's in this message," instructed the Chief, giving the clerk a five dollar gold piece.

"Yes, sir," barked the clerk as the Chief headed for the door.

Donnally and Bell were just finishing their breakfast when a Western Union errand boy came into the dining room. He looked around, spotted the pair, and came over.

"Mr. Donnally?" queried the boy.

"Being so good-looking always gives me away," said Eddie, making Bell and the boy laugh. After tipping the boy, Eddie and John looked at the telegram together.

Discreetly proceed STOP
Silver Creek. Right away STOP
Come prepared STOP
Can be found STOP
Frontier Saloon STOP
Chief STOP

The pair immediately left the hotel for the Denver office. Once there, they shared the telegram with Joe Walker.

"The next regular train is 7 a.m. tomorrow morning," said Joe. "We could probably get there on one of the mining company trains today, but it wouldn't be discreet. They all know me, and after one drink in Silver Creek, everyone in town would know we were there."

"The Chief said discreet, so tomorrow morning it is," said Donnally.

"You boys prefer rifles or shotguns?" asked Walker.

"We're city guys, Joe," said Bell. "We'll stick with the shotguns. You handle the rifle." Eddie nodded in agreement.

"If you guys can buy three tickets this afternoon, we can meet at a cafe a couple of blocks from the station between Sixth and Canyon Streets around 6:30. I'll have the guns in traveling cases, and we can get on separately, just in case somebody recognizes me," instructed Walker.

"Sounds like a plan," said Eddie. "We'll get out of your hair right now, then."

He gave his best smile to Miss Jenkins as they were leaving. She answered with a dismissive finger wave.

CHAPTER 44

Will got a good seat on the wooden sidewalk halfway up the street from the bank and got ready for a long wait. Mr. Stanley showed up a little before 9 a.m. He was actually one of the last to arrive. Lisa was right; you could see his vest from a block away. Another man that Will assumed to be the Vice President of the bank had actually opened the doors and let in the employees.

The morning passed without incident. The town was in a festive mood and nobody paid any attention to another cowboy lounging on the sidewalk. Will ate lunch at a cafe around the corner from the bank. Two other men, dressed like local businessmen, came in but Will didn't recognize either one. He had purposely waited until after the normal lunch hour. At four o'clock, the bank employees started leaving. Joshua Stanley stood at the door and let each one out with a friendly farewell. It was shortly after four when a man wearing an Army uniform came to the door. The man just appeared at the door and Stanley let him in. Will almost missed it, what with wagons and horses passing between him and the bank. He crossed the street to make sure he could see the officer when he left the bank. Will was fairly certain it was Captain Fairchild, the head of the Army Cavalry unit overseeing the delivery of the money and the transfer shipment of gold.

No other employees left the bank, and 30 minutes later, Captain Fairchild slipped out of the bank and headed toward the livery stable where the troops were quartered. There was no doubt who it was, and Will knew he had identified the last two pieces of the puzzle. Fairchild, however, was an older man, which Will found odd. Being a former army man, he knew most Captains were younger men intent on moving up in rank. Based on his age, Fairchild's army career was not going well for some reason. Maybe that's why he is mixed up in this business, reflected Will. He waited another fifteen minutes, and when Stanley left the bank, Will didn't bother to follow. He wanted to meet the others and didn't want to risk anything by following the crooked banker. Instead, Will walked up and down the main street looking for Carl or Albert. He figured neither Lisa, Schuster nor the Chief would be alone. He spotted Carl going into the hardware store alone and quickly crossed the street and followed him in. The store was crowded, but Will had no trouble working his way up to Carl and whispering, "Have everyone meet in the Chief's room at 6 p.m. It's very important."

Carl, to his credit, acted like he hadn't heard a thing and continued to look around the store. Will made his way back outside to kill some time until six o'clock.

Will took a seat in the lobby of the hotel and waited for everyone else to arrive. They all drifted in by six o'clock. Will waited a few minutes, then headed to the Chief's room. The door opened at Will's soft knock and Lisa flung herself into his arms. Will turned bright red while everyone else just grinned.

"I wish I had gotten that kind of welcome," said the Chief.

"I see you have all met each other!" exclaimed Will.

"Yes, and a fine group it is, but let's talk business. It's not like we have a lot of time. Obviously, there has been some development. Who has anything to report?" questioned the Chief.

"Me and Lisa didn't have much luck," replied Schuster. "As far as we could tell, everything around the hotel and restaurant seemed normal and legal."

The others, including the Chief, reported similar conclusions.

"I think I've got something," replied Will. "I saw the Cavalry Captain talking with Joshua Stanley, the President of the bank, after banking hours. Something tells me they're in on this deal. With those two in together, anything is possible in the way of an exchange. And now there are a total of at least seven bad guys we have to watch for."

"I really believe we should start watching the bank tonight just in case they try to make the exchange," chimed in the Chief. "If I were running this, I would want to make the exchange and get out of town. The closer it gets to the actual celebration, the more activity there will be around the gold and the money. The fellas from Denver will be here first thing tomorrow, so we just have to get through tonight."

Everyone nodded in agreement, except Lisa. "I don't disagree, but people are going to notice when none of us are around. Me and Uncle Frank are supposed to eat with Harry Cox, and I'm sure the Chief is spoken for."

"Yes, I'll be holding court at the Frontier Saloon," answered the Chief.

"You're right, of course," grinned Will. "Carl, Albert and me will watch the bank tonight. If something happens, one of us will come get the rest of you and the Sheriff. But we all need to be very careful. We have no idea where Andrew White and his two thugs are."

"Sounds good," replied the Chief.   "When do you think something will happen?"

"I'm not sure.   We're assuming they'll do this before the celebration and not after.   And I agree one hundred percent. The closer it gets to the actual day, the more crowded it will be around the bank.   Seeing that Cavalry Captain at the bank makes me think it might be soon," replied Will.

"The sooner the better," laughed the Chief, "but Lord give us one more day."

They coordinated everyone's whereabouts for the evening, and by seven o'clock or so, Will, Albert and Carl started moving into position around the bank building.   It was just getting dark, so they could hide themselves in the shadows fairly easily.   All three were wearing pistols, since anyone carrying a rifle in the vicinity of the bank would immediately arouse suspicion.

CHAPTER 45

The bank had a loading dock at its rear that was surrounded by a tall wooden fence. Will chose a spot where he could see the back alley and the gate. Carl and Albert were each covering a side of the bank, but Will believed the activity and the danger would be at the back of the bank. Will was just settling into a comfortable position when he was shocked to see the flare of a match from the gate. Will strained his eyes to make out a man leaning back against the gate. Despite the deepening darkness, Will was certain the man was wearing an Army uniform. Will knew in a heartbeat what was happening. The crooks had started making the exchange just before dusk so lights wouldn't be necessary. There would be no strange lights to alert anybody and nightfall would cover their departure. There was nothing unusual about an Army wagon moving around at night down main street.

Will slipped from his viewing spot and hurried to tell Albert and Carl. He quickly outlined the situation and Carl left to warn the others.

"We're going to have to try and stop them before they leave," said Will. "We have no way of knowing where they are in the exchange process. We'll try to take the hombre at the gate without the others knowing."

"I'll do my best to help you. Just tell me what to do," replied Albert.

"Hopefully, Carl will be back with the others real soon," said

Will. "You stay just a little behind me and we'll sneak down the alley and get the drop on the gate guard. The guard may not be involved, just assigned sentry duty by the Captain. Inside, there are probably four: the Captain, Stanley, Fredericks and Simpkins. They are all dangerous and would have no reservations about killing either of us, but they will be hesitant to fire a gun this close to the bank." Albert's knuckles were white where they were wrapped around his pistol, which was now out. Will gave him a reassuring clap on the shoulder. "Don't be afraid to shoot first," he said. They moved down the alley in unison.

Will would have preferred to surround the fenced-in loading area with Army personnel and order the outlaws out. But it was too late to worry about the way he wanted things. They were going to have to play the cards as they lay. But Will knew how dangerous this whole situation was, despite his warnings. Without the element of surprise and some luck, they were in trouble. They had no up-front Army support and there was an inside man from the bank. On top of that, he had no idea where Andrew White and his two thugs were. But Will knew they had to be close and were most probably inside the fence. Actually, he hoped they were.

Will eased down the alley, hugging the wall and staying in the deep shadow until he was about thirty feet from the gate guard. He retrieved two medium stones from his pocket that he had picked up earlier.

"You stay here and cover me," Will whispered. "But don't fire unless it's a life or death thing." Will lobbed the first stone down the alley and was rewarded by the faint whup of it landing in the dirt nearly thirty feet past the guarded gate! The guard stepped away from the gate and peered into the darkened alley opposite from Will. Will moved with the guard and halfway across the separating space, Will lobbed his second rock, which also landed with a soft thud down the alley. With his total concentration in the opposite direction, the guard never heard Will coming. In his last strides, Will drew his revolver and brought it down sharply behind the guard's right ear. Scott caught the guard's rifle on the way down and quickly dragged the crumpled figure away from the gate. With Albert's help, he trussed the soldier up with his own Army issued belt, gagged him with his bandanna, and stashed him around the corner of the fence. Will checked the man, and to his relief, found a steady pulse. It was always tricky hitting someone over the head with a revolver. If you do it too hard, you fracture the skull and kill the target. If you don't do it hard enough, you just make whoever you hit really mad, and a fight is sure to ensue. For Will, it was one thing to shoot someone when you had to, but altogether something else to hit someone from behind fracturing their skull and killing them in cold blood.

He took the soldier's revolver and stuck it in the small of his back under his vest. He took the rifle and laid it some distance from the downed Army man.

"What happens now?" whispered Albert.

"We wait here at the gate for the others to get here. With this guard gone, we control the only way the outlaws can come out," said Will. "You go up to the end of the alley and help Carl lead the others in and keep 'em quiet. Hopefully, all the crooks are inside, but we don't know for sure."

Albert left with a nod and a grin.

Will settled down to wait and started trying to find a space in the wooden wall where he could peer into the loading area. What I wouldn't give for Eddie, John and Joe, he thought.

When Carl left the back alley, he headed straight for the hotel to get Schuster and his sister. He leaped up the steps to the hotel and rushed excitedly into the restaurant, so excited that he nearly knocked over a waitress carrying a tray of suppers. With a burning red face, Carl located Lisa and Schuster and made his way to their table.

"Have a seat and join us for supper, young man. Any relative of Lisa's is welcome here," beamed Harry Cox. Carl hadn't expected this and didn't know what to say. His mind raced, and after what seemed like forever to him, he blurted, "Your horse is real sick and Will needs your help".

Lisa quickly stood up and said, "Supper will have to wait."

Dismayed at losing his beautiful supper guest, the hotel dandy exclaimed, "Who is this Will? Can't he doctor the dumb animal himself?"

"Oh, it's Will Scott, our hand, and if he says he needs help, he needs it!" exclaimed Carl before anyone else could reply.

At the sound of Will Scott's name, a man eating in the corner by himself scowled noticeably. While Lisa and the others were leaving, he paid his bill and slipped out the front of the hotel, leaving his half-eaten meal behind.

The trio went out the back of the hotel and started heading toward the saloon to alert the Chief.

"What's happening, Carl?" asked Lisa.

"The outlaws are loading the money behind the bank. Will and Albert should have done something with the guard that is in the alley by now. Once that was done, they were gonna wait for the rest of us to get there," replied Carl.

"I'll go in the saloon and alert the Chief," said Schuster. "We've caused enough commotion already. You two wait here."

In two minutes, Schuster was back, and in just a couple more minutes, the Chief himself strolled out. They all joined in a darkened doorway several stores down from the saloon where Carl quickly told his story. The small group hurried down the opposite side of the street from the bank.

CHAPTER 46

Meanwhile, peering through a gap in the fence, Will could see there were four men loading crates onto a double team freight wagon. They had lit one lantern, but it was not fully turned up. Will could see that they were almost loaded. He kept checking the alley for his reinforcements, hoping they would hurry up. He saw Albert step out of the shadows and wave. Will motioned them over.

"Chief, when we go inside, you and Albert go to the left and cover the wagon driver and anyone else you see. Frank and I will go to the right and get the drop on the others. Lisa, you and Carl go for the wagon team. I don't want them to try and bolt the open gate. Next time one of the horses moves a little, we'll go in," whispered Will Scott. "It looks like they are almost finished loading."

Will reached up and unlooped the leather strap that was holding the gate together. Fortunately for Will, the crossbar had not been reinserted by the outlaws since they had posted a guard outside. It was only a few seconds before one of the horses shuffled his feet, snorted, and shook his head, rattling his harness. Will swiftly opened the gate wide enough for them to slip through in single file. Their timing could not have been better. Two of the outlaws were locking the back door of the bank, while a third was bending over in the back of the wagon rearranging one of the crates. The fourth was starting to get in the driver's seat. The first any of the outlaws knew of their predicament was the mechanical ratcheting of Will cocking his pistol, which sounded loud in the near silence. "Nobody move. You men are under arrest," snapped Will. "Get your hands in the air."

The one at the door froze and then slowly raised his hands in the air. The one in the back of the wagon straightened up and his hands shot up. The other started to turn away from Will toward the other side of the wagon.

"You heard the man," growled the Chief, his large revolver plainly aimed at the outlaw's midsection. The man slowly raised his hands, seeing he was clearly outgunned. The man in the driver's seat didn't move, since he was looking down the barrel of Albert's gun.

"Frank, relieve these fellas of their hardware," instructed Will. Schuster moved forward and took a revolver from inside the banker's coat. He found a two shot derringer in a vest pocket. In addition, he removed a revolver from each of the other three men and found a boot knife on one of them.

"You fellas are real clever," growled Schuster. "You at the door, cross your legs Injun style and sit against that wall."

"Carl, could you and Lisa run get the Sheriff and bring him over?" asked Will. Carl left Albert holding the head of the horse team and he and Lisa hurried out the now half-opened gate.

"Okay, now it's your turn, fellas. Step down off the wagon but keep your hands high," ordered the Chief. The men had little choice but to do what they were told. He made the outlaws sit against the wall. Will stepped up on the raised loading dock and turned up the outlaws' lantern. The banker's face was ashen; the man was practically in shock.

"Do you want to tell us about the rest of your gang, Captain

Fairchild?" growled Will. "You are a disgrace to your uniform."

"I ain't telling you nothing. You people are interfering with official military business," blustered the Captain.

"Shut up," barked the Chief. "I can't wait to see you behind bars."

"This is Al Fredericks and Andrew White, Chief," said Will, gesturing toward two of the seated outlaws.

"Save your breath, Scott," growled Fredericks. "You should be as dead as that Mexican partner of yours."

Will's hand tightened on his pistol, and he struggled with the blind rage to kill the man named Al Fredericks, who had been a part of Miguel's ambush. Instead, he said, "Thanks, I didn't know for sure who shot Miguel. I kinda figured it was you and that partner of yours. Where is he, anyway, still out at the mine?" Will smiled inwardly at the astonished look on both White's and Frederick's faces when they realized Will knew about the mine.

CHAPTER 47

"**Y**ou're real smart ain't you, lawman?" came a voice from behind.

Will turned, and now it was his turn to be shocked. The big outlaw had his deadly sawed-off shotgun aimed directly at them. Carl's limp frame was draped over one shoulder. Lisa was standing next to him, her lips squeezed into a tight line. A gun barrel was jammed in her ribs and the hand holding it belonged to none other than Alvin T. Maddox, Secretary of the Treasury of the United States.

"Drop your gun, Chief, the rest of you too," snapped Maddox.

Will laid his pistol on the loading dock floor while Schuster, Albert and the Chief did the same. Nobody even thought about doing anything else. Between the double-barrel shotgun and the gun on Lisa, they had no choice. The four former prisoners scrambled off the floor and retrieved the newly dropped set of weapons as well as their own.

"Captain, you and Stanley get back over to the saloon and let people see you. We can continue with our original plan," instructed the Secretary. "I'll be there shortly. Fredericks, Simpkins and Andrew can handle this little group."

Before leaving, Captain Fairchild got right in Will's face. "I've dreamed about getting even with you for years, Scott. I was a Captain under Colonel Martin, and thanks to you I'm still a Captain. I've been stuck in all kind of places, always getting passed over for promotion, never able to get my own command and always snubbed by my fellow officers, all due to a bunch of ignorant savages."

Despite the situation, Will answered, "You were a disgrace then and nothing seems to have changed. I still regret not killing Martin that day."

"It would have been better for him if you had," snarled Fairchild. "Stuck up on the northern border, he started drinking all the time until one winter night he blew his brains out. I hope these boys make you suffer. I'm just sorry I won't be there." Fairchild turned and stalked out without looking back.

The shotgun toting outlaw dumped Carl in the back of the wagon, while the Secretary rudely pushed Lisa onto the loading dock.

"You know you're done for, Maddox," said the Chief. "Even you can't cover up all of us missing."

"That's where you're wrong. Nobody knows all you people are connected. I've seen to it that only very few people in Washington know about the counterfeit and nobody in this territory has a clue. You and Scott there will just be more operatives killed in the line of duty," laughed the Secretary. Fredericks, the thinner outlaw, moved among them waving his gun in each one's face.

"Now, I am going back to the saloon and have a drink. Have a nice trip," snarled Maddox, as he walked out the gate.

Will's mind had been racing while the Chief talked. He knew in his heart that the outlaws meant to kill them all.

"Killing all of us still won't ensure you won't be caught," argued the Chief.

"Nobody will find your bodies for years, mister," said

Andrew White. "The mine will be your final resting place. Some of you will just get there before the others," he growled, casting a leering glance at Lisa. "Now get in the wagon."

Simpkins motioned the Chief in first, then Lisa, Albert, and finally, Will. Simpkins kept them covered constantly with the sawed-off shotgun.

He settled himself across from them and propped his feet on Carl's still form lying in the bottom of the wagon. Simpkins leered at Lisa and said, "I can't wait to get you out to the mine, sweetie." His shotgun had moved slightly away from Will.

Will knew that everyone's fate rested on his ability to get to the gun he had in the small of his back. When he had knocked out the outside guard, he had stuck the man's revolver in his own pants. It was an unusual place for a gun in those days, and Fredericks had only been concerned with the gun in Will's holster that had been laid on the loading dock. In those milliseconds, he knew he couldn't let Lisa and the rest of the family be killed.

Will quietly turned himself sideways and frantically grabbed for the hidden revolver. He knew he didn't have a chance; his only hope was that any shooting would bring someone to investigate and save the others. The big outlaw saw Will's movement. He also knew Will didn't have a chance, and an evil grin appeared on his face as he swung the shotgun toward Will, knowing he had the advantage. Will's gun was clear, but in actions divided into frozen segments, he knew he was way behind. He saw it all—the evil grin, the looming barrels swinging his way with their impending doom, and his own gun halfway to where it needed to be. Everything was moving in slow motion by now, and his vision had tunneled down to only

Simpkins and the shotgun. The blood was rushing in his ears and he didn't even hear Lisa's scream.

In the next frozen moment, just before the two barrels lined up, Will saw two red splotches explode on the big man's chest. Then Will's gun was bucking in his hand and he could hear Lisa's scream, as well as the two shots he had just fired. The additional .44 caliber slugs took Simpkins off his feet and he flipped over the side of the wagon. Both barrels of the shotgun fired harmlessly in the air but with a tremendous roar.

"Do not move, Señor," Will heard, in a voice he knew as well as his own. He turned and saw Miguel standing inside the gate with his Winchester leveled at Al Fredericks.   While Will brought his pistol to bear on Andrew White, who was struggling to control the half spooked horses, the Chief stood up and removed weapons from the stunned outlaws and said, "You men are under arrest, again!"

Will stepped out of the wagon and over to where Simpkins lay. He didn't even bother to bend down to check; the evil grin was forever frozen in death.

Then Lisa was in his arms, the tears flowing down her cheeks. "I thought you were dead," she murmured.

"I thought we were all dead," he answered.

"You know I could just slap you for such a foolhardy thing you did," she said, stamping her foot and grinning through the tears. Will didn't really answer, just took her hand and rushed toward Miguel and a Mexican vaquero who was standing just behind Miguel with a pistol in his hand.

"Buenas noches, amigo," said Miguel, with a weak smile.

Will swept the Mexican off his feet with a big bear hug. "Am I glad to see you, amigo!" growled Will. "But how did you end up here?"

"The day everyone leave, Juan Velasco and two more vaqueros from New Mexico come with horses to breed. They told me they come up every few months with horses. I decided to come fight with you once more. I see the way you look at Señorita Lisa and the way she look back. I think maybe this is our last fight, and I want to be there," related Miguel. "We rode very hard since dawn."

"You saved me again, amigo," stammered Will, overcome with emotion.

"It was close. I had to wait for a clear shot. I knew there was no way you wouldn't do something," laughed Miguel. "I think maybe you have, how you say, used up at least one of your nine lives!"

Meanwhile, Schuster and Albert were tending to Carl, who was slowly coming around. Thankfully, Simpkins had only sucker-punched him, knocking him out cold. The Chief had the other two face down on the loading dock. Will couldn't hear the Chief, but he could tell it wasn't polite conversation he was dishing out.

There was a commotion in the alley as the town Sheriff, a large man in his fifties, and a gangling young deputy carrying a lantern arrived at the gate. They were accompanied by two lanky Mexican vaqueros.

"What's going on here?" blustered the Sheriff. "Who are you people?" The Sheriff himself was carrying a sawed-off shotgun and in his agitated state was not being real careful about where he pointed it.

"Sheriff, I think you remember me," spoke up the Chief, stepping forward.

"Yes sir," replied the Sheriff, eagerly identifying a familiar face. "What's going on here?" the Sheriff repeated.

"These two men, along with the Secretary of the Treasury, the Secretary of the Interior, as well as the bank president and Captain of the Army detail are being charged with violation of the counterfeiting laws," stated the Chief.

"Go ahead, Jimmy, and put the shackles on these two," instructed the Sheriff to his deputy.

The deputy quickly put a pair of handcuffs on White and Fredericks, who both appeared to be in shock.

"There is another one in an Army uniform tied up outside the fence that needs to go," added Albert.

"We'll have to question him. He may have just been posted as a guard and not told what the Captain was up to," said Will.

"Chief, I can't believe it!" exclaimed the Sheriff.

"Believe it!" barked the Chief. "In this wagon is twenty million in real greenbacks. In the bank is the same amount of some of the best counterfeit notes ever made. These fellas planned on making themselves some very rich hombres. If you could send for Colonel Wilcox, we'll have him and his men take custody of this money. We'll also need the undertaker for this one."

"Jimmy, you and these Mexican gentlemen, if they're willing, escort these two over to the jail and then stand guard there," ordered the Sheriff.

"We are pleased to be of assistance," replied Juan, the lead vaquero. "These people are our family."

Carl groaned in the back of the wagon and groggily sat up. Lisa rushed over to help her stricken brother.

"That was a fine thing you tried to do, Will," said Schuster, clapping Will on the back.

"We're not finished yet," replied Will.   "Let's go get the others. They think they are so stinking smart."

Lisa stepped away from Will and gave Miguel a big hug and mimed, "Thanks." She noticed his pallor and hoped he hadn't opened his wounds. She also grabbed Juan, who she knew well, and hugged him.

"Cancel that," bellowed the Chief.   "Will, I want you and Albert to take Miguel, Lisa and Carl back to the hotel. Me, Schuster and the Sheriff here will go get those others and put them in jail."

CHAPTER 48

It was hardly an hour before the entire group was reunited in the hotel restaurant with the Chief and Schuster. Carl had recovered except for a large knot on his jaw. After the adrenaline rush, Will was drinking strong coffee to keep going. They were all trying to question each other at once when the Chief held up his hand.

"I'm most likely the oldest, not counting Mr. Schuster, so I get to talk first. Miguel, how the dickens did you get here?" asked the Chief.

"I know it is muy importante that I be here to arrest los hombres. These vaqueros," he said, pointing to Juan and the cousins, "they come from New Mexico right after Señor Will leaves. I convinced Juan, Manuel and Diego to take a ride with me. We each brought an extra horse and swapped off." Looking at Lisa, he said, "The horses are fine, just tired. Louisa was very unhappy with me. It is my lucky day to be here just in time," he explained, "but I could never have made it without these three, not to mention Señorita Lisa's horses."

"No, it was our lucky day!" exclaimed Will. "How did you know where we were?"

"I came to see the bank and we were coming down the street just as the Secretary and the big man slugged Carl and grabbed Lisa. After that, it was easy. I was just waiting to get a clear shot at the big man when you started all the fun," laughed Miguel. "You don't always have to be first, mi amigo."

"I still don't understand these vaqueros from New Mexico," said the Chief. "And thank you very much, by the way."

"Every few months, Don Ramos Gonzales, from Alcalde, New Mexico sends up some brood mares to breed with Lisa's horses at the ranch. They usually take back several yearlings and some geldings. They just happened to come now, thank the Lord," explained Schuster.

"Tell us what happened with you, Chief," chimed in Lisa.

"Well, we found that scoundrel banker and the dishonorable Captain on the first floor of the saloon. When they saw us and the Sheriff, they were too shocked to try anything. The deputies took them out of a side door of the saloon straight to jail. The two big shot politicians were upstairs buying drinks for everyone and having a big party. They never even saw what happened downstairs," said the Chief. "It was really special. The two were so busy being big shots that me and the Sheriff practically had them in handcuffs before they saw us. Their big party ended real quick."

"I'm going to have Eddie, Joe and John question the whole sorry bunch tomorrow and find out the whole story. After a night in jail, I'm sure at least one of them will tell the whole story," added the Chief. "The Sheriff has a very unique jail here. He has a separate jail building with individual walled cells. It seems these miners like to drink and brawl, so after they break up the fights and arrest them, he puts them in individual cells. He said if he didn't separate them, they'd just start fighting all over again. Our friends are all isolated. Besides, the Sheriff's Deputy, Colonel Wilcox, has a whole platoon surrounding the jail building. The money and the counterfeit are inside the bank with another platoon around it. "I don't care about the rest of you, but I'm packing it in," said Schuster. "I'm sure we'll all be talking with the Sheriff in the morning."

"Quite right," exclaimed the Chief. "I'll be there first thing, but right after breakfast all of you should come over. Eddie, John and Joe will be here first thing. They are going to be mad they missed all the fun, and I'm sure they'll take it out while questioning the prisoners."

"Just hold on, Chief. This is my case, and it's my responsibility to question these outlaws," stated Will with firm resolve.

"Look, son, humor an old man, will you? I don't get to do this very often and I want to make the most of it. You look after the young lady, her family, and that Mexican partner of yours," instructed the Chief. "I've commandeered some rooms for the vaqueros. I'm going to the Western Union Office and send a telegram to the President and the Assistant Secretary of the Treasury. Unfortunately, because of the celebration, there are all kinds of newspaper people here. Two cabinet Secretaries are not arrested every day, and this thing will be in the papers back East pronto. I really don't want the President to see it in the paper before he hears it from me."

As if on cue, they all left, and it was Will and Lisa, alone in the deserted restaurant.

"You know, I am just now realizing how scared I was tonight," she said, putting her hand in his. "I don't know how you do this work."

"I think it's just something that kinda comes natural," said Will, "not the shooting or killing part, but the hunting and tracking part. Having to kill someone even though there is no choice is something you always carry with you."

"Aren't you always scared?" asked Lisa.

"No, not really. I was scared tonight, but not of dying. I was scared that I wasn't going to ever get to be with you like this again. That's a new idea for me. We usually move on after a case," replied Will.

"Well," she said, "you could move on."

Will's head snapped up and his face mirrored the anguish in his heart.

"Or you could come stay with me at the ranch for a while," she replied with a big smile.

"For a while?" he answered with a big smile, leaning forward to give her a lingering kiss that put the night's events out of their minds.

The only thing they could think of was each other and the unsatisfied passion they had controlled. Control was forgotten on the way to Lisa's room, and the rest of the clothes that hadn't been removed going up the stairs disappeared with the closing of the door. Maybe it was the anticipation or the close brush with death, but their entire world consisted of only each others' bodies and the intense physical pleasure they were giving each other.

When the Chief arrived at the Western Union Office, it was bedlam. There must have been a dozen newspaper men, and they were pushing and shoving and calling for the clerk to open up. The Chief could see the young clerk, who had wisely locked the door, standing behind the counter wringing his hands.

"What's going on here?" the Chief bellowed, freezing everyone in place.

The group quickly recovered and began shouting questions at the Chief. The Chief held up his hand. "This is how it's going to be, gentlemen. I will give you a brief description of an official investigation, and you will be free to communicate that with whomever."

"Currently under arrest for violating the counterfeit laws of the United States are Secretary of the Treasury Maddox, Secretary of the Interior Stang, one Army captain, the President of the Bank, as well as two other men. One additional individual was shot and killed by Secret Service Operatives. Now, I'm going to send a message to the President, giving him an accounting of our investigation. When I come out, I expect you gentlemen to have worked out among yourselves the order telegrams are going to be sent out. Our investigation is ongoing, but rest assured, the 20 million in genuine currency and the 20 million in gold bars are completely safe. The celebration will continue as scheduled."

With that, the clerk, who had been listening, opened the door and the Chief went in.

CHAPTER 49

By the time Will and Lisa came down the next morning, the restaurant was as deserted as it had been the night before. They quickly downed some hot coffee and leftover biscuits and rushed over to the Sheriff's office. As they stepped into the office, all eyes turned to look. Everyone was there: the Chief, the family, Miguel, the vaqueros and the Sheriff. It was hard to tell who was the darker shade of red, Will or Lisa. Fortunately for them, the Chief was still in command.

"For your information, Operative Scott, this case is completely solved. I have a complete account of this scheme right here in writing. I don't think any of these hombres will be on the loose again for quite a spell," replied the Chief.

"Who talked first?" asked Will.

"The Sheriff and I started with the banker, Joshua Stanley," said the Chief.

"A night alone in a jail cell completely unnerved the man. He's a swindler and cheater, not a tough guy. He couldn't talk fast enough," added the Sherriff. "He has been doing land swindles and cheating people for several years. He went to school back East with Bill Stang and Maddox but really wasn't part of their activities back then. He became involved with White out west here. White is Maddox's cousin, and he was always the muscle for their little gang. Maddox was always the brains behind all their schemes, but it was a string of coincidences that let them hatch this thing," advised the Chief.

"This celebration was a legitimate thing, but the Secretary got lucky," continued the Chief. "The two printers are German-speaking Swiss, and they got detected stealing at the Bureau of Engraving and Printing. One is a pressman and the other an engraver. That event is what inspired Maddox to concoct his plan."

"According to Stang," said the Sherriff, giving the Chief a chance to catch his breath, "Maddox had White and Simpkins come back East and convince the Swiss brothers their only way to escape jail was to come West for a printing job. The Swiss brothers didn't really know it, but they were coming one way or the other. White promised them their freedom and one million of genuine currency."

"Simpkins, the one you killed last night, and Fredericks, had done a lot of rough stuff for the banker and Andrew White in the past, like burning ranches, beating people up or making them disappear, so the banker and White could get their hands on valuable land."

"Former Secretary Stang, better known as dumpling over at his office, also couldn't talk and write fast enough," added the Chief. "He got a lot of encouragement from Eddie Donnally."

"Fredericks knew he was in deep for shooting Miguel, and of course, blamed it all on White, Maddox and the dead Simpkins," continued the Sheriff. "He made a full confession to John Bell."

"They kill the poor Swiss brothers, Chief?" asked Miguel.

"No, fortunately, they just turned them loose here in town. Being Swiss and speaking with a German accent, they stick out something awful, and no one would believe their wild story even if they told it to somebody. They are in a room over at the livery stable, being guarded by Sheriff's deputies. They are also talking, but in their excitement it is half in German," said the Chief. "I think they know how lucky they are to be alive."

"What happened to the cook?" asked Will.

"Unfortunately, if I understood them right, the last they saw him, he was headed toward the mine with Simpkins," replied the Chief. "With Simpkins dead, we may never know exactly why he did away with the cook and let the brothers go."

"What about those first bills that showed up?" asked Will.

"Well, it seems that one of the wagon drivers helped himself to some of the notes. The Swiss brothers ultimately noticed some was missing, but only after this fella was gone. At the time there was no one around for them to tell except the cook. The banker spotted the counterfeit notes at the bank but couldn't get to them before they were shipped out. He told White, and White sent Fredericks and Simpkins after this driver, but he had already spent some of the money," explained the Chief.

"I assume this driver's bleached bones are in some canyon around here," mused Schuster.

"Actually, the brothers said that Simpkins and Fredericks showed up one afternoon in a wagon and dug two graves. They never saw the bodies, but later they noticed the mounds of dirt were flat, but weren't about to ask any questions. I'm guessing the driver must've shared his newfound wealth with a friend," advised the Chief.

"What about the Army Captain?" asked Will.

"As he told you, he's been out West for a number of years

and unknown to the army, he engineered some shady land deals with the banker and Andrew White," answered Chief Taylor. "It was just dumb luck, but everything lined up right for this bunch. Maddox arranged for him to be added to Colonel Wilcox's troop when they got here. Everything was going their way until we found those first notes and you and Miguel started working the case," advised the Chief. "As you know, Fredericks and Simpkins ambushed you, but fortunately the two of you were not together. They were committed to killing you two, but Maddox didn't want it done until the last minute. He knew that if I learned you two had been killed, I would flood this area with operatives, the Army, and the U.S. Marshals. By the way, I wired Denver last night and six U.S. Deputy Marshals are headed this way with a prisoner transport wagon. The Army has taken custody of the Captain, and with his past record he is in danger of a firing squad. Most people don't know it, but the only crime mentioned in the Constitution besides treason is counterfeiting," finished the Chief.

"How's your head, Carl?" asked Will, changing the subject.

"It's fine. "It would take a harder knock than that to break my thick head," laughed Carl. "Besides, it's my jaw that's sore."

All of a sudden, the room got real quiet as three hard-looking men came in.

"Top of the morning," said Eddie, giving Lisa an engaging smile. "The Chief has told us all about you!" Eddie gave Will a wink.

"And Will has told me all about you, Mr. Donnally," answered Lisa, offering Eddie her hand.

"Come now. It's Eddie. We're practically family," laughed Eddie.

"These other two fine gentlemen are John Bell and Joe Walker," said the Chief, making introductions all around.

"You'll notice I didn't call this one a gentleman. He's Irish, and when he leaves, you should check your wallet," added the Chief.

"Chief, I guess I need to have a word with you," said Will.

"Yes, I would expect you do," mused Chief Taylor.

"We'll meet you down at Lewis' Store," murmured Lisa, as she and her family trooped out the door. Miguel and the vaqueros slipped out of the door without a word.

The Chief gave a nod to the three operatives, and they trooped out, too. Eddie left last, frowning at Will.

"I think I'll go check on the brothers," said the Sheriff on his way out.

CHAPTER 50

"Chief," said Will, searching for the right words. "Look, son. Let me tell you something. I know you're leaving the Service. I knew it the first time I saw you and that girl together. It's the right time and place for you. Besides, I'm not going to be the Chief forever. I'm always making some politician or another mad, and arresting Secretary Maddox and Secretary Stang won't help any. The politicians are all for law and order, except when it is some of them being investigated and arrested. When I leave Washington, I think me and Miss Lucy will just head on out here to stay. Denver is really growing and turning into a real city," advised the Chief. "Besides, Schuster has invited me to the ranch for a deer hunt and a big party," grinned the Chief.

"I'll be here to make sure these crooks are taken care of properly while you head back to D.C.," affirmed Will.

"Darn right you will. I'm not doing all your work for you!" said the Chief. "But Joe can handle most of it."

While Will was having his word with the Chief, Lisa and her group were having some words of their own.

"What do you mean, you're going away?" asked Lisa, rooted to the wooden boardwalk.

"Tell her," said Carl.

"You know the only reason I came back to the ranch was to help you. I love the ranch, but I'd much rather stayed back East. Chief Taylor offered me a position with the Treasury

Department, and I'm going to go back East," said Albert.

"And I'm going, too," chimed in Carl.

"What?" asked Lisa.

"Well, if Will would recommend me, maybe I could go to that Virginia Military College," said Carl.

"You know we always wanted him to go to school back East. Now I'll be there to look after him some," said Albert.

"Well, what have you got to say?" Lisa said, stamping her foot and glaring at Schuster.

"I'm not going anywhere but home. I think these two have you outnumbered, though," said Schuster.

"Well, I know when I'm beat," she smiled, and gave them both a huge hug, wiping away some tears. "When are you two planning on leaving?"

"I'm going in a week or so," said Albert. "Carl can wait until the next school term. We need to make arrangements, but I'll take care of all that when I get to Washington."

"Now that that's all settled, let's go load up the wagon," growled Schuster. "I ain't taking on no hired help yet."

"We're not leaving before the Celebration, are we?" asked Carl.

"No way," said Lisa. "I think we all need to relax and enjoy ourselves."

After his talk with the Chief, Will went searching for Miguel. He found him in a Mexican cantina near the livery stables hunched over a plate of huevos rancheros and talking in Spanish to the three Mexican vaqueros that had helped the night before.

"Buenos días, mi amigo," greeted Miguel. "Es finite, no?"

"Yes, it's all done! The outlaws are in custody, but I'm

staying out here for some of the court work. This bunch is bound to have some slick lawyers. The banker, Secretary Stang and Fredericks talked, and the Chief thinks the Captain will testify if offered the right deal," advised Will. "The Swiss brothers have also given statements and will probably receive leniency. Maddox and White will probably fight to the end, but the evidence is overwhelming."

Miguel groaned, knowing the boredom that went with assembling evidence and preparing for court, even if he didn't have to testify.

"We are going back to the ranch, no?" asked Miguel hopefully.

"I must have my thoughts written on my face," said Will, shaking his head. "You and the Chief amaze me. The Chief is getting John and Eddie to go with the Army out to the printing site and gather evidence. We are off the hook."

"We are destined to be together, mi amigo. According to my friends here, Señorita Louisa is a very good matchmaker and she has many muy bonita nieces. I think I can make, how you say, beautiful music together with one of them. I am one handsome hombre. I also think we can raise the most beautiful horses, if you will take me as a caballero."

Will reached out and grasped Miguel's outstretched hand. "You'll never be a caballero for me. We've always been partners, and partners we'll stay. I don't know how we'll arrange it, but we can figure out something." Miguel was too choked up to reply and Will's throat wouldn't allow him to speak further. The bond between them was once again sealed forever.

After the incident with Miguel, Will went looking for his

fellow operatives and found them in a corner of the hotel dining room. He pulled up a chair.

"Now, let's see," said Eddie Donnally. "You leave me with Pinky McFadden in D.C. and you come out here and end up with a fine lady. Don't you know the Irish are supposed to be lucky?"

"No luckier than an honest Scotsman," said Will. They all laughed together.

"This was one heck of a case, and we could never have done it without each other," said Will. "But you all know that I'm going to have to give up the life."

"Shucks," said Joe. "We all want to give it up, but we're all good at it, so it has to be something special to leave for and it looks like you have found it."

"You're one of the best," said John Bell. "We'll miss you. Hopefully, you and Lisa will come back East for a visit now and then."

"I'm sure we will," said Will.

"Pinky McFadden will sure be happy to hear the news," Eddie laughed. "You better get back to Lisa before she comes to her senses and comes looking for an Irishman."

Will shook hands with each of them and then took Eddie's advice.

CHAPTER 51

The sun was setting over the rim of the canyon and the dying rays bathed the valley with an orange hue. Will and Lisa were sitting on the porch in big rocking chairs. In the six months since the confrontation in Silver Creek, the contentedness of their being together just kept getting stronger.

"I'm looking forward to trailing the horses down to New Mexico," said Will.

"I've always loved it," sighed Lisa, "ever since I was a little girl. It was always a great adventure."

"I actually miss Miguel, "said Will.

"Don't feel sorry for him," exclaimed Lisa. "From what Louisa has heard through the grapevine, Miguel has become the Don Juan of New Mexico."

"You know I've been thinking maybe of going back to the Texas hill country for a spell to see my brother," said Will. "I'm supposed to be his partner, you know?"

Lisa snorted. "Humph, you traveling men are all alike, worrying about what's over the next hill and not paying attention to the here and now."

"We could go soon and be back in plenty of time for the trip to New Mexico," said Will.

Lisa frowned. "I'm not sure proper people back East would approve of me, a single young woman, traveling around with a vagabond like you."

"Don't worry yourself about that too much. I've already

asked Uncle Frank's permission, wired your brothers, Miguel, Eddie, the Chief and my family, that we're coming to Stanclift Farms for a wedding celebration. That is, if you'll have me?" he sheepishly queried. "I guess maybe I should have asked you first."

Lisa let out a squeal that didn't stop until she was in his lap with her lips pressed against his. "You are the devil, Mister Will Scott, but my mother always said, the only thing the devil ever needed to make him decent was a good wife!!!"

Epilogue

The trio was shocked and surprised as their doom buggy entered the exit area of the Haunted Mansion.

"How did we get here?" exclaimed Stephen.

"I have no idea," said Maggie. "Let's get some place private where we can talk."

They hurried out the exit door.

"Let's go to the cemetery again," said Lizzie. "It's quiet there."

When they got to the cemetery, the trio went straight to the tombstones and stared down at a familiar one. But this time, it read: "Here lies Slim Johnson, hung for his dastardly deeds, too many to mention."

"I don't even know where to start," said Maggie, "and I'm afraid to ask, but do either of you know Will or Miguel?"

"Now I know what Ace meant," marveled Stephen. "It was like I was a part of Will. I could see and hear exactly what was happening and kind of feel things."

"Me, too," said Lizzie, "but I was with Miguel. I didn't hurt when he was shot, but I was right there with him the whole time."

"I was with Lisa," said Maggie, incredulously. "I was there too, seeing and feeling almost everything." She and Stephen both blushed.

"What?" asked Lizzie.

"There were some adult things between Lisa and Will," said Maggie.

"I kind of went to sleep during some of that," stammered Stephen.

"Me, too," said Maggie, "but I could feel the love they had for each other."

"Yeah, I could feel that, too," admitted Stephen, grudgingly.

"Look," she said, pulling from beneath her shirt a heavy silver chain with a large turquoise nugget.

"That's Lisa's," said Stephen. He felt something warm in his pocket, reached in, and pulled out a silver Secret Service badge
"I've got Will's badge."

"I've got something too!" exclaimed Lizzie, pulling a gold chain out of her shirt. They looked closely and could see that it was a gold Mexican coin.

"Look at my back," said Lizzie. "I can feel something warm."

"Maggie lifted the back of Lizzie's shirt, and she and Stephen stared with their mouths hanging open.

"You've got a scar where Miguel was shot!" exclaimed Stephen.

"It's not a real scar, Lizzie," assured Maggie. "It just looks like a thin straight line. Does it hurt?"

"No, but I just know it's there," replied Lizzie.

They all looked at each other, and Stephen expressed their shared question. "How are we going to explain all this?"

"We've got to get to Mimi before we see anyone else. She sent us to that trunk. She must know Ace!" exclaimed Maggie.

Lizzie was texting Mimi before Maggie had even finished. "I told Mimi we needed to see her right away, and I asked her if she knew anyone named Ace."

"Geez, Lizzie. If she doesn't know Ace, we are all headed for the looney bin!" exclaimed Stephen.

Lizzie's phone chimed as Mimi answered in text, "Ace is a friend of mine. Meet me at the corner table at the cafe in Tomorrow Land."

The trio turned and started to jog toward their rendezvous.

"Okay," said Maggie. "Let's just slow down, take some deep breaths and not draw any attention to ourselves."

"Good idea," said Stephen, as he and Lizzie slowed to a walk.

The kids saw Mimi as soon as they entered the cafe. She was smiling as they hurried over.

"I'll show you mine if you show me yours," said Mimi, as she pulled out a beautiful gold medallion she had around her neck. The medallion glowed slightly.

The trio all pulled out their mementos, which were also slightly glowing.

"I guess you three had quite the adventure," said Mimi.

"It was really something. It was just like Ace said. We were living history!" exclaimed Stephen.

"Can you explain all this, Mimi?" asked Maggie.

"First, let me tell you that our mementos are just that, ours. Only someone that has been through the Mystical Mouse Gate can see them. If you see someone, and yours feels slightly warm, you'll know they have been through the Mouse Gate, too," explained Mimi.

"Is Ace really a leprechaun?" asked Lizzie.

Mimi laughed. "I guess he is. Everything he says always seems to come true. I'd say we have to take him at his word since I have no idea how a person could check."

"Can we talk about our trip?" asked Maggie.

"Sure," said Mimi. "Abuelo and I have some good stories for you, but we'll have to wait until we get home and can be alone together. He's keeping everyone else busy while I came to meet you."

"Abuelo knows Ace, too!" exclaimed Stephen.

"Very well," said Mimi. "They always share a drink of Irish whiskey together when Ace comes to visit, but only one. I'm scared of what a drunk leprechaun might do," laughed Mimi.

"We'll let you read our journals when you get home," said Mimi. "They are on the very top shelf in the office."

"Wait," said Maggie. "I have ours right here in my backpack."

She pulled it out and opened it. The three children gasped in unison and Mimi smiled.

"It's in English, and we can read about it over and over," gushed Lizzie. "I don't know about you guys, but my history ended with Miguel in a cantina."

"Mine ended when Lisa was headed for Will," said Maggie.

"And the last I remember is that Will was headed for Lisa, when we got to the end of the ride," added Stephen.

"I can't wait to read it and then talk about it with you," said Mimi, pulling them all into a big hug. "I also have a little surprise for you. There are more journals in the trunk, and they are all in leprechaun. I don't think you've seen the last of Ace!"

An article that appeared in the 1901 issue of Strand magazine, which pertains to the Secret Service and shows images of seized evidence and the USSS Headquarters.

STRAND
April 1901

Secret Service.

By George Grantham Bain.

THERE are secret service divisions in almost all of the great departments at Washington, but what is known as *the* secret service is the one which is connected with the Treasury Department. This service has to do with the detection of the counterfeiting of money. It also guards the person of the President of the United States. The President goes forth from the Executive Mansion almost every morning for a walk or a ride, and not infre-

One of the most remarkable cases in the history of crime in the United States is that of William E. Brockway. He has just been released from prison after serving a term for forgery committed at the age of seventy years. Former Chief Drummond says that Brockway had no moral sense of the wrong of counterfeiting.

"My bills are finer specimens of workmanship than those in circulation," he said once to Chief Drummond, "and I consider that any man has a right to make all the

CHIEF WILKIE, OF THE SECRET SERVICE BUREAU, IN FRONT OF THE CABINET OF PHOTOGRAPHS IN THE ROGUES' GALLERY.

quently he is quite alone ; but usually there is a secret service officer not far away. His chief duty is to protect the President from cranks or persons with a slight mental twist, rather than from the malicious or criminal.

Where the secret service finds its greatest activity is in the pursuit of the makers of counterfeit money. It is an extraordinary fact, stated to me by a former chief of the service, that an expert engraver who could earn a large income legitimately will stick to the business of counterfeiting when once he has undertaken it : he cannot be reformed.

money he wants to if he can make it as good as the Government engravers do."

Brockway had a theory that no one was the loser by the circulation of counterfeit money so long as the fraud was not discovered. He said that the bill circulated just like a Government note, and that if a man could spend it he was not harmed by taking it in place of a genuine bill.

Brockway has served many terms, but for some of his greatest crimes he has never done a day's time. What the Government thinks more important even than the punish-

SECRET SERVICE.   281

THE MUSEUM IN THE SECRET SERVICE BUREAU OF THE TREASURY DEPARTMENT.

October, 1880, two officers of the secret service arrested Doyle as he was leaving the New York train at Chicago. He had been shadowed all the way from New York. In his valise were two hundred and four thousand dollars' worth of Government bonds–all counterfeits. Brockway and Smith were arrested in Brooklyn on the following day and Smith turned State's evidence. But

ment of the criminal is to get possession of his counterfeit plates. Counterfeiting is almost invariably done by a gang of men. If only one of the confederates remains at large, and the plates have not been captured, they can be used for further fraud. Or, if all the gang has been captured, on its release it can again begin the manufacture of counterfeit money with a full equipment immediately. The counterfeiter without his plates is harmless for several months, if not for a year or more.

The most remarkable crime in Brockway's history was the counterfeiting of U.S. Government bonds of the face value of one thousand dollars each. His associates in this crime were men named Martin, Foster, Doyle, and Smith. They were known as expert counterfeiters, and they were constantly under the eye of the secret service officers, but this did not prevent them carrying on their dishonest business. In
Vol. xvi.—36.

Brockway held a trump card. He knew where the steel and copper plates used by the counterfeiters were concealed. He offered to surrender them if released. The authorities agreed to this, and he gave minute directions where the plates were buried. There were twenty-two of them, including plates for a one hundred dollar National Bank note and plates for another one thousand dollar bond, from which no prints had been made. With these were

COIN MOULDS CAPTURED FROM COUNTERFEITERS.

COUNTERFEITING OUTFIT CAPTURED BY THE UNITED STATES SECRET SERVICE.

and ten dollar bills, and he began to raise his own notes by cutting the figures from the bills of broken banks, which were then as common as good ones in the middle West. He was very successful in doing this, and this encouraged him to attempt something greater in his chosen criminal career. He got acquainted with Ben Boyd, who was a finished engraver, and took lessons from him until he became skilled in the work. Then he hired out to a firm of counterfeiters. The head of this firm was a prominent citizen of Cincinnati, a Church member and a member of the School Board. McCartney married, and accumulated something like twenty-five thousand dollars, after which he settled down in Indianapolis as a horse-dealer. But a quiet life did not agree with him, and he began counterfeiting again. He was arrested many times, and made many escapes which were famous in the annals of the secret service. Many of these were procured by bribery.

fifty thousand dollars in counterfeit, one hundred dollar notes, and several hundred sheets of fibre-paper. Brockway did not serve a day in prison for this crime.

The audacity of the man was illustrated by his choice of notes and bonds of such large denominations for his work. Hundred dollar notes and one thousand dollar bonds do not circulate among the ignorant or those easily imposed upon. But it was a fact that Brockway's plates were almost, if not quite, as good as the Government's. Three years later Brockway was caught in another counterfeiting scheme. This time he was forging one thousand dollar bonds of two railroads, and on one set of these he had forged the London stamp. Experts said it was impossible to detect these counterfeit bonds. Brockway got only five years for this crime.

Pete McCartney was one of the men famous in the history of the secret service. Strangely enough, McCartney got his education from a family of counterfeiters. Their name was Johnston. William R. Johnston, who was McCartney's companion, had been convicted of counterfeiting, and so had his brother, his father, and his grandfather. The Johnstons were small counterfeiters, for they confined their attention to one dollar bills. McCartney did business in Illinois in the time when railroading was unknown. He carried his stock in a wagon. While doing this it occurred to him that he might just as well pass five dollar

Brockway, McCartney, and Ogle were princes in the criminal community. From these men who dealt in hundreds of thousands it is a gradual descent to the Italian—he is often an Italian—who makes a crude cast of a piece of silver in plaster of Paris, and turns out rough pewter coins, a few at a time, which he passes on the ignorant in the foreign quarters of great cities like New York. There are all grades of counterfeiters, and the little ones are, of course, the most numerous. They are captured sometimes in odd ways.

Only a short time ago a man working on a Government building in a Western city by the merest chance saw a man at an adjacent window apparently filing the edge of a coin. This man, as it was proved, had a counterfeit in his hand, and was trying to imitate the milling on the edge of it. It was only a chance that he was engaged in anything illegal, but the workman reported the matter

SECRET SERVICE.   283

to his employer, the secret service people were notified, and an investigation resulted in the capture of a small band of counterfeiters of no great importance.

The laws against counterfeiting are much more severe and comprehensive than they were a few years ago, and sometimes their execution goes to what seems a ridiculous extreme.

Some years ago a New York newspaper issued a "guarantee of circulation," offering to forfeit a certain sum if its claims proved inaccurate ; and the engraving and colouring of this certificate closely resembled the Government securities. It was used by criminals to defraud the newly-arrived immigrants who could not read the inscription, but who recognised the dollar-mark and figures following it and thought it was valuable. These and similar frauds were the occasion for the passage of the law which is now enforced so strictly. Its enforcement results each year in the seizure of a large quantity of advertising matter as well as wagon-loads of printing presses, plates, and counterfeit money in various stages. All this is kept in a small room adjoining the office of John Wilkie, the chief of the secret service. Mr. Wilkie's office is in the Treasury Building. In it is a rogues' gallery and specimens of counterfeiting hanging on the walls.

There is a novel form of occupation growing out of the crime of counterfeiting. There are men who go from city to city giving instructions to bank clerks in the art of detecting false money. These men have counterfeit bills in their possession which they hold by virtue of a permit from the Secretary of the Treasury. Every bank has one or more of these bills to use as object-lessons.

The most remarkable case which has come under the eye of the secret service in many years was the conspiracy to defraud the Government by the use of counterfeit stamps on cigar-boxes. This business was carried on between Philadelphia and Lancaster, Pennsylvania, and the U.S. Attorney for the eastern district of Pennsylvania and his assistants were involved in the conspiracy. All the principals in this conspiracy were punished, and the Government officials, Bingham and Newitt, were convicted of trying to bribe a secret service officer and sentenced to two and a half years each in the penitentiary. Jacobs and Kendig, the principals in the case, were fined five thousand dollars each and sentenced to two years' imprisonment. In this conspiracy were involved manufacturers as well as Federal officials, and the capital employed was in the hundreds of thousands.

CHIEF WILKIE, OF THE UNITED STATES SECRET SERVICE, IN HIS OFFICE.

A Mouse Gate Adventure Book
What's your adventure?

CPSIA information can be obtained at www.ICGtesting.com
Printed in the USA
LVOW13s2312271013

358795LV00002B/101/P